FROM THE NANCY DREW FILES

THE CASE: At first the pirates were content to steal yachts . . . but now they've resorted to kidnapping.

CONTACT: Ned's friend David Peck is the son of a wealthy and prominent member of Belizean society.

SUSPECTS: Manny Mai—*A local involved in protecting the native habitat, he may have gone outside the law to save the land from outsiders.*

Ramón DaSilvio—*He claims to be an anthropologist, but to Nancy he seems more of a con man than a man of science.*

Becca Jackson—*She's beautiful, clever, and as dangerous as they come. She has her eyes on Ned . . . and perhaps a great deal more.*

COMPLICATIONS: Manny Mai. Becca Jackson. Nancy Drew. Ned Nickerson. Jealousy and suspicion. Slow dances and slow burns. There are complications in every corner and in every heart.

Books in The Nancy Drew Files® Series

Available from ARCHWAY Paperbacks

The NANCY DREW Files™

108

CAPTIVE HEART

CAROLYN KEENE

AN ARCHWAY PAPERBACK
Published by POCKET BOOKS
New York   London   Toronto   Sydney   Tokyo   Singapore

AN ARCHWAY PAPERBACK *Original*

An Archway Paperback published by
POCKET BOOKS, a division of Simon & Schuster Inc.
1230 Avenue of the Americas, New York, NY 10020

Copyright © 1995 by Simon & Schuster Inc.
Produced by Mega-Books, Inc.

ISBN: 0-671-88199-X

First Archway Paperback printing June 1995

10 9 8 7 6 5 4 3 2 1

NANCY DREW, AN ARCHWAY PAPERBACK and colophon are registered trademarks of Simon & Schuster Inc.

THE NANCY DREW FILES is a trademark of Simon & Schuster Inc.

Cover art by Cliff Miller

Printed in the U.S.A.

IL 6+

CAPTIVE HEART

Chapter

One

"NED, HI!" NANCY DREW WAVED happily as she stepped out of the airplane and spotted her boyfriend, Ned Nickerson, waiting for her on the open balcony of the small airport.

Ned brushed his wavy brown hair off his forehead and blew her a kiss. "Welcome to Belize," he called.

The tall, blond young man standing next to Ned waved to Nancy with enthusiasm. Nancy was fond of David Peck, who, as an exchange student, had stayed with Ned and his family the previous fall while he attended a semester at Ned's college.

As Nancy hurried down the platform steps she felt the heavy, hot tropical air, sweet with the scent of flowers. She was glad she had changed on the plane from sweater and slacks into a light cotton dress.

Once inside the airport, she passed through immigration and customs, eager to be in Ned's arms once again.

"Nancy!" Ned swept her up when she was free at last. He whirled her around and finished the greeting with an enthusiastic kiss. "I'm so glad you finally wrapped up your last case. I thought you'd never get here."

Nancy laughed. "So did I." Her shoulder-length reddish blond hair framed her pretty face. "Hi, David. It was so nice of you to invite us to visit."

David shook her hand warmly. "Ned and I have been having a good time, but now that you've arrived, we'll really celebrate."

"Get ready, Nan," Ned said as he loaded her luggage in the trunk of a red sports car. "David and his friends have parties planned day and night. It sounds like he'll be introducing you to almost everyone in Central America."

David opened the door and Nancy slipped into the soft leather passenger seat of his car. "And why not?" he said with a grin. "I can't wait to show off such a charming and lovely girl."

Nancy blushed slightly at the compliment, but had to admit she enjoyed David's enthusiasm. His family, originally from England, had been one of the first to settle Belize when it was called British Honduras, but sometimes his style

2

seemed more flamboyant Latin American than reserved British.

"It will be fun to meet your friends," Nancy responded, smiling at him.

David waited for Ned to fold all of his six feet two inches into the tiny backseat of the sports car, then turned on the engine. "Tonight we'll start slowly, since you might be tired from the trip. We're having dinner with my best friend, Manny Mai, whom I've known since our first year in school."

"You'll like Manny," Ned promised. "He's a Mayan Indian, a really interesting guy."

"Sounds great," Nancy said. "The Mayan culture is fascinating, and I'd love to learn more about it."

David laughed as he headed for the airport exit. "You'll probably learn more about boats than about Mayans from Manny. He's the proud owner of a twenty-footer that he uses to take tourists out fishing, or to Hol Chan for snorkeling."

"Hol Chan is a marine park," Ned explained. "It covers a mile of the reef, plus a huge chunk of lagoon and a lot of mangrove swamps. The Belizeans are trying to protect the natural beauty of the country."

"I can't wait to go snorkeling," Nancy said. "Is it true that you have the second longest coral reef in the world?"

David nodded. "Only the Great Barrier Reef

in Australia is longer. You'll be amazed at the variety of coral and fish you'll see. If you want, I'll fly you out to our family's island, Cay Casa, tomorrow. It's right on the reef."

Nancy noticed that he pronounced the name of the island "Key" Casa. "Great! Do you have your own plane?"

"Well, it belongs to the family," David replied modestly.

Ned had told Nancy that David's large family was prominent in Belize. They owned property all over the country, raising everything from sugarcane to oranges to cattle. In addition, his father and one of his uncles held important positions in the government.

After leaving the airport, David headed toward the coast. Nancy noticed the variety of houses lining the road: tiny cinder block bungalows, thatch-roofed huts on stilts, modern stuccos painted in pastel shades. Often a well-kept home, beautifully landscaped, would be flanked by wooden shacks with chickens, goats, or horses grazing in the yard.

She could see Belize City to the south as David turned into a narrow dirt lane that led across the flat savanna land to what appeared to be a grove of palm trees. As they drew nearer, she realized that under the shade of the palms was a large, pretty Spanish-style house with sprawling verandas and gardens.

"Welcome to Casa Playa," David said.

"It's lovely," Nancy said. She caught a whiff of sea breeze, a welcome cooling tonic for her damp skin. Although it was only spring, it seemed like a hot August day back home in River Heights.

"My parents are away on business," David said, "but they'll return tomorrow." He asked the housekeeper to show Nancy to her room. Marie, plump and cheerful, led Nancy to one of several guest rooms on the second floor. It was spacious, with French doors that opened onto a covered veranda.

Nancy stepped onto the balcony and took in the spectacular view. She saw a swimming pool surrounded by gardens of tropical flowers and the shallow, aqua blue sea beyond.

"It is not now the rainy season," Marie said in a lilting Creole accent. "You can leave the doors open. The bugs have not yet come."

"I may do that," Nancy said, as she stepped back inside the room. "Is there a beach?"

"No, not here," Marie said. "Only a sea wall. The beautiful beaches are to the south."

After a quick shower, Nancy joined Ned and David on the lower veranda for a glass of freshly squeezed orange juice from the Peck orchards. Soon it was time to leave for dinner. They drove to a nearby village and parked in front of a small restaurant.

"It's not very fancy," David said as he led them inside, "but the food is first-rate. Good, there's Manny."

A well-built young man with a broad face and a mop of thick, straight dark hair jumped up from a table when they approached. As Nancy shook his hand she realized he wasn't much taller than her five feet seven, but she could sense the power of his muscles rippling under his golden brown skin.

"Welcome to Belize, Ms. Drew," Manny said, his dark eyes sparkling with humor. "How do you find our country so far?"

"A bit warm," Nancy answered, laughing. "But fascinating. I'm looking forward to seeing all of it."

"David must fly you to Ambergris Cay soon, so I can take you out on my boat." Manny held her chair while Nancy sat down. "Do you like to scuba or snorkel?"

"I love both."

"Later I will take you down to the Blue Hole for scuba, but first you must snorkel at Hol Chan." Manny's eyes shone with pride. "You'll be amazed at what you'll see."

The waiter arrived, and Manny ordered for all of them. He charmingly refused to translate his choices for Nancy, saying he wanted to surprise her. When the food arrived, she was delighted with the delicious, unfamiliar flavors.

"This is wonderful fish," Nancy said after tasting it. "What kind is it?"

"Yellowtail snapper," Manny said. "I caught it myself this afternoon and gave it to the chef before you arrived."

"It's excellent." She sampled another dish. "And what kind of meat is this?"

"Do you like it?" Manny exchanged a glance with David, trying to hide a smile.

"I do. The sauce is great." Nancy caught the gleam of mischief in Manny's eyes. "So what's the secret?"

"Should I tell her, David?" Manny teased.

"No, let her enjoy her meal." David played along with Manny's game.

"Come on, 'fess up, guys," Nancy said.

"If you're sure . . ." Manny winked at David. "It's eel." He sat back to wait for her reaction.

"Is it?" Nancy said calmly. "I've had eel before, but it didn't taste this good."

A sudden silence followed. Nancy glanced at Manny. He was staring at her, astonished.

David burst into laughter. "She got you, Manny, and good. Come on, admit it."

Manny shook his head, beginning to smile. "All right, you win. I can see she's not like most of the tourists I deal with."

"You're right, she's not." Ned had been watching with great amusement. He knew that Nancy had eaten fried rattlesnake, alligator stew, and a number of other unusual dishes during her career as a detective. "She's not like *anyone* you've ever met before, Manny."

"Yes, I can see that." Manny, still smiling, gazed at her with an unspoken emotion smoldering in his dark eyes.

Nancy wondered what he was thinking. She

felt slightly uncomfortable but also strangely excited by the mystery hidden behind his handsome face.

"Hey, did you hear the news?" David asked Manny. "They think another yacht was attacked by pirates. It disappeared just off the coast."

Manny gave David a sharp look. "You're kidding. Here, near Belize?"

"That's right," David said. "This makes four yachts missing. From what the radio report said, it sounds like the same gang, although they changed their method of attack slightly."

"Are you saying there are pirates operating in the Caribbean?" Nancy asked, her curiosity aroused.

"Yes, the first yacht was stolen near the Cayman Islands several months ago," David told her. "It was anchored in an isolated cove overnight, and everyone was asleep. The pirates sailed up in a small boat and boarded the yacht so quietly the people on board were blindfolded before they knew what was happening. Ten minutes later they were cast adrift in a life raft, watching their yacht sail off without them."

"It sounds like the same gang," Manny said. "Each time it's been so quick and smooth it's over before anyone can react. The only thing that changes is the way the boats are boarded. The second time, near Jamaica, it happened in broad daylight. Everyone had heard about the first capture, so most yacht crews took turns standing guard each night."

"No one expected them to attack during the day," David explained. "This time they used a larger sailboat. The pirates were beating into the wind—you know, tacking back and forth."

Nancy nodded. "Ned and I sail, so we know what you mean."

"The target yacht was on a steady course, running wing and wing before the wind."

"So the boats were headed toward each other?" Ned asked.

"That's right," David said. "The pirates crossed in front of the yacht, then suddenly tacked and cut behind the stern. There were only two people on board—a man and wife. He was dozing on the forward deck, and she was at the wheel. She screamed, but before she could turn the yacht, one of the pirates leapt on board with a line and tied the two boats together. By the time the man got back to the cockpit, the pirates had a gun pressed to his wife's head, and all he could do was surrender."

"That's awful," Ned said. "What about the third hijacking?"

"That was south of Haiti," Manny answered. "This time the target was a big cabin cruiser. Since the first two captures were of sailboats, the crew wasn't too worried. They were out fishing when they spotted an old wooden boat bouncing around on the waves, its sails flapping. They watched it for a while but couldn't see anyone on board. Finally they decided to check it out, thinking maybe someone was hurt or had been swept overboard. The moment they tied up, the pirates swarmed out from below deck, and it's the same story all over again."

"Do you know any details about the yacht that disappeared near here?" Nancy asked David.

"Only that it was to arrive in Mexico. The wife of one of the men on board reported her husband missing. Apparently he always phones home the moment they make port so she won't worry. When she didn't hear from him, she called the Coast Guard."

"Have they begun a search?" Nancy asked.

David nodded. "Yes, though they're fairly sure the victims are all right. One good thing about these pirates is that they never hurt anyone, and they stock the life rafts with plenty of food and water before casting them adrift."

"But that's not the weirdest part," Manny added, leaning forward. "Believe it or not, the pirates first go through a strange ritual. Each man on the yacht has his right ear pierced!"

"What?" Nancy blinked in surprise.

"Isn't it incredible?" David said. "They may lose their boats, but they gain solid gold earrings."

"Wow." Ned touched his right earlobe as if he were protecting it from being pierced. "That's really bizarre. Only the men? Not the women?"

"Just the men." Manny leaned back, enjoying their reactions.

"You're a detective, Nancy," David said. "Can you figure it out?"

Nancy shook her head slowly. "No, but it's a very intriguing story."

"Maybe you should investigate," Manny suggested.

Nancy laughed. "No, thanks. I'm here to enjoy Belize, not take on a new case." She raised her glass of papaya juice. "Here's a toast to your lovely country and to a visit full of just plain fun."

"I'll drink to that." David clinked his glass against hers. "Fun it shall be."

Early the next morning, David flew Nancy and Ned in his amphibious plane to Cay Casa. Manny couldn't join them because he had a fishing charter to take out that day and had returned to his home on Ambergris Cay the night before.

David landed on the water and taxied up to the dock in front of the house, a rambling building with white walls and a red-tiled roof. Like Casa Playa, it was surrounded by lush tropical plants and flowers. A strong breeze blew steadily from the east, bending the coconut-laden palm trees.

"What's the matter, David?" Nancy noticed his frown as he helped her up onto the dock.

He studied the water. "I'm afraid it won't be a good day for snorkeling or scuba diving. This wind has the water all stirred up, and you won't be able to see much."

"That's too bad." Nancy was disappointed, but she wanted to save her first view of the coral

11

reef for a day with good conditions. She noticed Ned looking at a sailboat tied up at the dock, and she walked over for a closer look. It was about eighteen feet long with an open cockpit and a small sail locker up in the bow.

"What a great little boat," Nancy told David. "If we can't snorkel, why don't we go for a sail instead?"

"Good idea!" David seemed pleased that the day of fun he'd planned wasn't going to be ruined. "I'll ask our cook to pack us a picnic lunch, and we can take the *Honeybee* out beyond the reef."

A short while later the three sailed off. Nancy took the tiller, and with David's advice she skillfully guided the boat through a gap in the reef and headed out to the open waters of the Caribbean Sea.

It was a perfect day for sailing, with a steady, strong breeze and a bright sun in the cloudless sky. Eventually they opened the picnic basket and feasted on lobster salad sandwiches, mangoes, and icy-cold fresh orange juice.

Ned took the tiller after lunch, and Nancy was adjusting the angle of the sail to catch the wind when she noticed a tiny object on the horizon.

"David, do you have binoculars on board?" she asked.

"Sure." He opened a locker and handed them to her. "See something?"

"Yes, but I'm not sure what." She focused the lens and scanned the water. The seesawing movement of the *Honeybee* as it cut through the waves made it difficult to look, but she finally located the object.

"Ned, we have to come about at once!" Nancy shouted. "It's a life raft, and I'm sure I saw at least one person in it."

They quickly altered course and raced toward the raft. Nancy kept the binoculars trained on it, and as they drew nearer she reported, "I see two people. Both are men, I think."

"The missing yacht had two men on board," David said. "Do you think we've found the pirates' latest victims?"

"I can't tell yet." Nancy studied the raft as they closed the distance. "They appear to be in good shape," she said.

Just then something glittered in the sunlight. "Wait a minute!" Nancy cried. "It looks like one of the men is wearing an earring. David, you were right, I think we've found the men attacked by the pirates!"

Chapter

Two

"HELLO!" THE LARGER of the two men on the life raft called when Nancy, Ned, and David came within shouting distance. "We sure are glad to see you."

"Are you all right?" Nancy called back.

"We're fine now." He whooped with joy.

Ned carefully steered the *Honeybee* up to the raft. The two men eagerly grabbed the line Nancy tossed them. They were sunburned and in need of a shave but seemed full of energy.

"Thanks," the big man said as David helped him board the yacht. "I knew my wife would send help," he told the smaller man. "Thank you, Beth." He blew a kiss into the sky.

His friend, short and wiry, waved off David's assistance and scrambled into the *Honeybee*'s cockpit. "My yacht is missing, all right," he said.

"That gang of miserable thieves hijacked the *Windchime*. I'd like to throttle their scrawny necks."

"So you *were* attacked by the pirates," Nancy said. "Please, sit down. Would you like some orange juice?" She opened the thermos.

"Thank you." The larger man sank down on one of the cockpit cushions and sighed with pleasure. "Ah, civilization. How I missed it."

David tied the raft to the *Honeybee*'s stern, then held out his hand. "I'm David Peck, and these are my friends, Nancy Drew and Ned Nickerson."

"Joe Mason," the big man said, shaking David's hand. "And this is Robert Cutler."

Cutler perched on the edge of his seat, watching as Ned turned the boat toward Cay Casa. He gave a brief nod. "Pleased to meet you. Thanks for the rescue."

"Nancy's the one who spotted you," David said, adjusting the sails to the new course. "You can relax now. We'll be back at the island in no time."

"You must have quite a story to tell," Nancy said as she handed them glasses of juice.

"Do we ever!" Joe Mason took a sip and sighed again in contentment. "This tastes fantastic."

"Did the pirates leave you supplies, as they did with the other rafts?" Nancy asked.

"Yes. Wasn't it kind of them?" Robert Cutler said sarcastically. "A few miserable rations in exchange for my *Windchime*."

"Now, Rob, take it easy," Joe Mason said. "They'll be found sooner or later, and you'll get your boat back."

Cutler shook his head. "It was my own stupid fault. How could I fall for such a trick?"

"What happened?" Nancy asked.

"It was about sundown," Cutler said. "We came across an old, rusty fishing outboard, and they signaled us. One guy kept pointing to the motor and shaking his head, obviously telling us they had engine trouble. I should have ignored them and sailed right past."

"How could we?" Joe Mason said. "Night was coming, and we were out in the middle of the ocean. We had to help a boat in distress. That old bucket of bolts looked as if it would fall apart and sink if the smallest squall came up."

"So you stopped to help, of course," Nancy said. "You can't blame yourselves for that."

"Maybe not," Cutler said, "but I should have had my gun ready. I knew about the pirates, and I kept a .45 in the cabin. A lot of good it did me. A gun's not much use below when the pirates are outside boarding you."

"Come on, Rob," Joe Mason said. "Neither one of us suspected those guys. I'm as much to blame as you are."

"I am the captain, and I was responsible," Cutler said bitterly.

"What did the pirates look like?" Nancy asked.

"There were four of them," Cutler replied.

"All quite small, almost small enough to be kids—"

"But they weren't kidding around," Mason interrupted, chuckling at his own joke.

Cutler looked annoyed. "They wore hats, loose pants, and long-sleeved shirts. They could have been men or women. Dark hair, brownish tan skin, from what we could tell."

"We didn't see their faces," Joe Mason explained. "Three of them had their backs to us as we pulled up to their boat. They kept their hats pulled down low and the leader wore dark glasses —the reflecting kind. He was the first one on board."

"He was as quick as a cat," Cutler put in. "One second he was bent over his engine, the next second he was on the *Windchime* with a gun at my head."

"And then the other three were all over us, wearing what looked like ski masks, only made of cotton," Mason said. "They slipped those masks on and jumped aboard before I could catch my breath. They were extremely quick and agile."

"Can you guess where they were from?" Nancy asked.

Joe Mason chuckled. "We've been arguing over that for the past three days—nothing much else to do while we floated around. They could have been Hispanic, Asian, or from any of the Caribbean islands."

Nancy smiled. "That doesn't exactly narrow

17

the field, does it? What about their voices—did you recognize an accent?"

"Nope." Mason grinned. "We've been arguing about that, too. The only one who spoke was the leader, and he didn't say much except 'please.' "

"Are you sure it was a man?" Nancy asked.

"Pretty sure," Mason said. "His voice was rather deep, and I think he had a Spanish accent—"

"—but not one I've ever heard," Cutler said. "And I've been cruising the Caribbean for three months. Joe only joined me a week ago."

"Yeah," Mason agreed. "Four days of luxury, three days of raft."

Nancy decided she liked this man. "No one else in the gang said anything?"

"They didn't need to," Mason said. "It was like a choreographed dance. Each one knew exactly where to go, what to do, and when."

"Of course, while we were blindfolded," Cutler added, "they might have communicated with hand signals. We only saw them for a few seconds before they tied scarfs over our eyes."

Nancy thought a moment. "You said the leader said 'please' a lot?"

"Oh, yes," Cutler said, sarcasm creeping back into his voice. "While he was stealing the *Windchime* and casting us adrift, he was extremely polite."

Joe Mason nodded. "It was weird, almost eerie. But I guess we're lucky we didn't get hurt—except for the holes in our ears, of course."

Nancy glanced at the simple gold ring in Mason's ear, then looked at Cutler. "I noticed that you're not wearing yours."

"Are you kidding?" Cutler said. "First thing I did sitting in the raft, watching the *Windchime* sail away without me, was throw the ring in the ocean."

"I told him it was a mistake," Joe Mason said with a wink. "He should have kept it as a souvenir." He touched his. "It's probably worth a lot of money, too. I'm not so rich that I can afford to feed solid gold to the sharks."

"Admit it, Joe, you love your ring. I always said you were a hippie at heart." Cutler spoke for the first time with a trace of humor.

Ned and David had been listening with fascination to the conversation. Now David stood up and scanned the horizon. "We're coming up on Cay Casa." He turned back to the two men. "Hot showers and cool breezes are just ahead, gentlemen."

Mason grinned. "As my daughter would say, all *right!*"

Cutler stared glumly at the waves breaking against the reef and the small island. "I just hope they're taking good care of the *Windchime,*" he muttered.

As soon as they docked at Cay Casa, David took the men into the house while Nancy and

Ned lowered the sails, tidied up the *Honeybee,* and secured the raft. When they reached the house, they found David on the radio phone to the police, reporting the safe return of Cutler and Mason. He then called his father while Nancy and Ned went out to wait on the shaded patio.

"Nancy, you've got that 'detective' gleam in your eye," Ned said as they settled into comfortable chairs. "You've stumbled onto a new mystery and you're interested, aren't you?"

Nancy laughed. "So, you noticed. You have to admit, these pirates are a fascinating puzzle. So polite, so careful to store food and water for the victims. Not exactly a bloodthirsty bunch like in all the adventure stories. And the ear-piercing really intrigues me."

They discussed the pirates until David and Robert Cutler, who was wearing borrowed clean shorts and a shirt, came out onto the patio. "Mr. Mason's calling his wife," David told Nancy and Ned. He turned to Robert Cutler. "Mr. Cutler, my father has invited you and your friend to stay with us until you're ready to leave Belize. The police and the Coast Guard will probably want to question you, and my father wants you to be as comfortable as possible while you're here."

"I'm grateful," Cutler said. "That's very kind."

"Mr. Cutler," Nancy said. "I know how much you want to get the *Windchime* back. I've had some experience as a detective, and I might be able to help. Would you mind if I inspected the life raft?"

"Look all you want," Cutler said with a weary wave of his hand. "I paid a lot of money for that life raft, but I hope I never see the blasted thing again."

Nancy and Ned went down to the dock, where they'd secured the raft with double lines. Nancy climbed in and began to look it over inch by inch. She found flares, fishhooks, a medical kit, and enough food and water for two weeks at sea.

Probing under the rubber bumper in the stern, Nancy found a small electronic object. "Ned! Does this look like a homing transmitter to you?"

Ned peered down from the dock. "It sure does."

"Come on." Nancy pulled the small gadget free of its Velcro fastening and led the way back to the patio.

"Mr. Cutler, do you recognize this?" she asked the wiry, intense man.

"No. What is it?" He peered at it, frowning.

"A homing device. It emits a constant signal so anyone tracking the raft will know its location at all times. I found this hidden in the stern."

"I've never seen it before," Cutler said. "And, as a safety precaution, I checked the raft and its contents only a couple of days before we were hijacked."

"Then I'm guessing the pirates put it there,"

Nancy said. "And since they know where the raft is—"

". . . they know where we are." Cutler finished the thought for her. "Let's dismantle this thing and get to the police before the hijackers get to us."

Chapter

Three

Ned disconnected the wiring in the homing device, and a short while later David flew everyone back to Belize City, on the mainland. They drove straight to the police station, where Nancy turned the transmitter over to a stern-faced sergeant, and they were questioned about the rescue. She thought about telling the police she was a detective but decided against it. She wasn't working on a case; she'd just happened to spot the life raft out on the ocean.

Nancy was signing her statement when David's father, Kevin Peck, arrived to see if he could be of service. Nancy was impressed by the tall, distinguished man with dark hair graying at the temples. The police officers showed him great respect as he smoothly guided Cutler and Mason through the various formalities.

"It's getting late," David said when he, Nancy, and Ned finally left the station and headed out to Casa Playa in his sports car. "Jerry Waters's party starts soon. We'll just have time to change our clothes."

"This is the first of the big bashes David promised you, Nancy," Ned said. "Some people are coming from as far west as Belmopan and San Ignacio."

"And Jerry told everyone to bring all their friends," David added. "It should be a blast."

"Sounds terrific," Nancy said. "I hope it will take my mind off pirates for a while."

The sun was setting when they parked in front of the Waters house, a stately white colonial. The skirt of Nancy's pale pink lace-trimmed dress swirled around her shapely legs as she got out of the car. Her reddish blond hair curled in gentle wisps against her cheeks, and although she'd used a strong sunscreen, her skin was lightly tanned by her day in the tropical sun.

Following the sound of reggae music, David led Nancy and Ned down a path to the garden. Bright paper lanterns cast a warm glow over the crowds of young people who danced on the patio around a large turquoise pool. Two large buffet tables overflowing with food were at each end of the patio.

"There's Jerry," David said, waving at a tall, lean redhead. "Come on, I'll introduce you."

Jerry stood by a table loaded with sliced papaya, watermelon, mangoes, bananas, and pineapple arranged in artistic patterns.

"So we meet at last, Nancy Drew," Jerry said after David made the introductions. "Ned and David have told me a lot about you, but they didn't mention how enchanting you are."

"Jerry speaks an untruth," David said to Nancy. "We described you to perfection." He turned to his friend. "Did I not say she was as lovely as a hibiscus blossom?"

"You make mock of her comeliness," Jerry responded. "I'd term her a rare orchid, so delicate are her charms."

Ned grinned at Nancy. "Don't mind them. They both belong to the Shakespeare Club and tend to get a little carried away at times."

"Common dolt!" Jerry laughed, giving Ned a friendly slap on the back.

A petite young woman with high cheekbones and a deep tan appeared at Jerry's side. Her lustrous dark hair rippled in waves down her back, and her red silk dress clung to her shapely figure.

Jerry turned to the girl. "May I present another American, Miss Becca Jackson, from the state of Louisiana."

The girl held out her hand to Nancy. "It's a pleasure to meet you," she said in a soft southern accent. Then her exotic, almond-shaped brown eyes swept over David and Ned and she smiled. "A real pleasure."

"Becca is cruising the Caribbean," Jerry said. "I gather it's both a business and a pleasure trip."

"Yes," Becca said. "My daddy owns some land that turned out to be just floating on a sea of oil." Her self-mocking laugh was surprisingly hearty for such a tiny girl. "So he asked me to take a look around down here, see if y'all have a piece of property or two where he can invest some of that nasty old cash that just keeps pouring in."

David winked at her. "Tough problem you have. But you've come to the right spot. Belize is a young country. We've been independent only since 1981, and we have a lot of growing to do. We need new jobs and new investors."

"So I've been told." Becca selected a slice of papaya and delicately bit into it. Her movement was as graceful as a swan's.

Nancy noticed that all three men, including Ned, were fascinated by her. Nancy was surprised. Ned didn't usually look at other girls with such interest.

"What other countries have you visited in the Caribbean, Ms. Jackson?" Ned asked.

"Oh, call me Becca, please. My, we've been just about all over. Daddy gave me this big ol' cabin cruiser to ride around in and we've been to St. Lucia, Martinique, Guadeloupe—just about every island there is."

Nancy studied the heiress. While she seemed to be bragging about her father's wealth, her tone of voice was slightly sarcastic, as if she were making fun of herself. Nancy wondered if she was embarrassed by being so rich and this was her way of dealing with it. "I notice you said 'we,'" Nancy said. "Are you traveling with friends?"

"No, it's just me and my crew. I was about worn out with all the social life at home. I told Daddy I just had to get away for a while, so here I am—at another party!" Becca laughed again, a deep chuckle.

Several new guests arrived, and Jerry made the introductions. David asked Nancy to dance, and a few moments later she noticed that Ned and Becca had joined the crowd moving to the reggae beat. Tiny Becca had to tilt her head far back to look up into Ned's brown eyes.

Jerry cut in on David and swept Nancy off around the pool. When the song ended, he introduced her to some friends who invited her to join them at the buffet table.

As the evening passed, Nancy had a wonderful time talking and dancing with a number of interesting new people whose skin colors ranged from pale pink to amber, copper, bronze and deep ebony. The Belizeans welcomed her warmly and asked her many questions about the United States.

Nancy noticed that Becca was equally popular, especially with the men. She flirted with all of them, sprinkling her favors around evenly. Nancy was also aware that Ned seemed to be at Becca's side rather frequently, even when Becca didn't pay special attention to him. She threw herself into each dance no matter who her partner was, and her frequent bursts of laughter rang out in response to many different remarks.

Nancy found the girl fascinating, although she wasn't too happy with Ned's reaction to her. Late in the evening, she watched Ned and Becca dancing to a slow, dreamy song. She felt slightly uneasy for a second, then she told herself Ned was only having a bit of innocent fun. And besides, she thought, they'd probably never see Becca again after the party.

But later she found out she was wrong. After the band played its last number, Ned strolled over to her. "Becca has invited us to lunch aboard her cabin cruiser tomorrow. Would you like to go?"

"I'm not sure," Nancy said, hedging. "David may have plans for us."

Ned grinned. "Nope. I checked with him and he said he'd love to come."

"Well, all right." Nancy told herself she had nothing to worry about. Even if Becca was very rich and very pretty, Nancy was sure she could trust Ned.

The next morning a young Coast Guard officer came out to Casa Playa to interview Robert Cutler, Joe Mason, and their rescuers. They all gathered in the living room and the officer introduced himself as Lieutenant Hamilton. He said he'd just arrived on a boat that had been patrolling the waters off the coast of Mexico.

"American, are you?" Joe Mason said, surprised. "I didn't realize our folks were in the Caribbean."

"Yes, sir, we are," Lieutenant Hamilton said. "When a U.S. citizen or vessel is in trouble, we're here to help."

"Well, that's good news," Robert Cutler said. "Do you think you can find the *Windchime—and* the pirates. I want to get my hands on those scoundrels."

"We'll do our best, sir," the officer said politely. "Why don't you start at the beginning and tell me how they managed to board your craft."

As Nancy listened to the story once again, her curiosity about the pirates grew. She decided that she would read up on the other hijackings as soon as she had a chance. The library was sure to have back issues of the newspapers, she figured.

By the time Nancy, Ned, and David described how they had found the life raft, it was almost noon and time to leave for Becca's lunch party.

They drove down to the harbor and found Becca's boat, *La Moola,* a gleaming white cabin cruiser. Thirty feet long, it was spotless, with polished brass fittings and an oiled teak deck.

"I'm so glad y'all could come," Becca said, greeting them. She led them into an air-conditioned salon. It was luxurious, with thick carpet, rosewood paneling, and plush chairs. The damask-covered lunch table sparkled with crystal and silver.

"This is my friend Ramón DaSilvio," Becca

said. "He's an anthropologist." She giggled. "That means he studies people."

A slender, suave-looking man stood up. He was of medium height, with dark hair carefully slicked back from his forehead. "The pleasure is mine," he said, with a slight bow.

"Ramón is an expert sailor," Becca went on. "He's making his way around the islands by crewing on various boats while he collects information for his paper on the Caribbean people."

"What is the subject of your paper?" Nancy asked.

"I'm studying the variety of races." His voice was deep, flavored with a light Spanish accent. "These islands are truly a melting pot of people from all over the world. I'm most interested in how the island populations differ from one another."

David whistled. "That's quite a job. There are so many islands with so many combinations of races."

Ramón nodded. "But by now I've become rather good at guessing a person's roots. Take Becca, our beautiful hostess, for instance." He cocked his head, studying her for a moment. "I would think that, in addition to Northern European, you have a combination of Spanish, African, and Native American blood, and possibly Incan, but definitely not Mayan."

Becca blinked her exotic eyes at Ramón for a second, then she laughed, a hearty chuckle. "You're partly right. My daddy is pure American and my mama was born on the island of Majorca in the Mediterranean Sea. Majorca's Spanish, so you got that right. And her daddy was from Kenya. But there aren't too many Indians—Incan or Mayan—cruising around Europe."

Ramón smiled wryly. "Well, I didn't say I was correct about everything."

A young Chinese boy, possibly twelve years old, appeared in the doorway and nodded at Becca.

"Thank you, Chang," Becca said. "Lunch is ready. Shall we sit down?"

Just as Chang, serious and proud in a starched white jacket, began to serve the soup, Nancy noticed the boat's motors begin to hum.

"Are we going somewhere?" Nancy asked.

"We sure are. There's no point in sitting at a stinky ol' dock," Becca said. "I told Lee Po—he's my captain—to take us out for a ride. Won't that be fun?" She beamed at her guests.

Soup was followed by fresh fish and vegetables in a tangy sauce, then chicken with fried plantains, a bananalike fruit. Chang served the courses with perfect manners and Nancy noticed that Becca seemed very fond of him, often giving him little nods of approval or else one of her sweet smiles.

Nancy began to relax and enjoy the meal when she noticed that Ned didn't seem as taken with Becca's charms as he had been at the party the night before. He and David were both caught up in Ramón's anthropology work.

31

"I come from a small town in Cuba," Ramón explained in answer to one of Ned's questions. "But I have always been interested in understanding the world. When I was a boy I found in the library a book by Margaret Mead, who studied the young people of Tahiti. I was most fascinated. . . ."

Nancy was too stunned to listen to the rest of his story. She'd read Mead's book, too. The title was *Coming of Age in Samoa.* Samoa, not Tahiti. Was it possible Mead had also done a study of Tahiti? Nancy was almost certain she hadn't. How could Ramón make such a mistake? It seemed impossible that a trained anthropologist wouldn't be completely familiar with Mead's groundbreaking study.

She looked at Ramón more closely. He was suave and sophisticated but seemed almost too smooth. When they'd been talking about sailing a few minutes earlier, it was clear Ramón knew a great deal about boats, but not the name of the last winner of the America's Cup. A sailor who didn't follow that race was like a politician who didn't know who'd won the presidential election. Yet Ramón was so glib that Nancy suspected no one else had noticed his lack of knowledge.

After Chang served dainty pastries and coffee, they all went out on deck. The hot sun was a surprise after the cool dimness of the salon, and the sea breeze was welcome. Here and there, small islets rose from the aqua blue sea.

"Lee Po, I think I'll take the wheel now." Becca

strolled over to a thin Chinese man who was steering *La Moola* through the shallow crystal-clear water. "My goodness, it's so bright out here. Would you be a darling and fetch me my sunglasses?"

Lee Po gave her a long, hard look, then said brusquely, "I am captain of the boat."

Becca's eyes flashed sparks of fire. "I said I wanted to steer for a little while. I'm certainly capable of such a simple chore. And you are capable of getting my sunglasses."

Lee Po stared straight ahead for a moment, his body rigid. Finally he said through gritted teeth, "Yes, ma'am."

No one spoke until he disappeared into the cabin. Nancy was amazed that an employee would talk back in such a way to the boat's owner, but she noticed that Becca kept her cool.

"Well," Becca said with a small laugh. "Why don't y'all make yourselves comfortable?" With a wave of her hand, she indicated the deck chairs.

Nancy sat next to Ramón. Ned and David kept Becca company at the wheel until Lee Po returned with the sunglasses. Then Lee Po took the wheel again and Ned, David, and Becca moved to the stern, talking about investment possibilities in Belize. Nancy was sure that Ned wasn't really as interested in banana and cotton plantations as he pretended.

Nancy turned her back on him and faced the Cuban. "Mr. DaSilvio . . ."

"Call me Ramón, please," he said with a smile.

She brushed windblown curls off her forehead. "Like the others, I'm fascinated by your work. If you've been here almost a year, you must have seen many of the islands."

"Oh, yes, but if you don't mind, I'd rather talk about you," he said. "Those who go on about themselves can become such bores, do you not agree?"

Nancy nodded, noticing that Ramón was playing nervously with a small round object he'd pulled from his pocket. He kept the object hidden in his palm, but she caught a glimpse of gold or copper and thought perhaps he was fingering a lucky coin.

Ramón smiled at her. "Becca tells me that you and your friends recently had a most fascinating experience. Is it true that you rescued the survivors of the latest pirate attack?"

"Yes, we happened to be sailing nearby when we spotted their raft," she said.

"I would like to hear about it," Ramón said. "These hijackings have been the talk of every island. When the first one occurred in the Caymans, most of the people I met thought it was only an isolated incident, but when it happened again near Jamaica, some people actually put out to sea in a hopeless attempt to find the pirates."

Suddenly Ramón dropped the round object he'd been playing with. He quickly picked it up but not before Nancy got a glimpse of it. It wasn't a coin. It was a gold earring, a simple band about half an inch in diameter—almost identical to the one the pirates had put on Joe Mason!

"It sounds like you were in the Caymans, and then later in Jamaica, when the piracies occurred. Is that true?" Nancy kept her tone casual, but she was studying Ramón's left ear. Yes, she could see the tiny scar left where the hole for the earring had closed up.

Ramón shrugged. "By chance."

"And now you're in Belize," Nancy said. "Were you also in Haiti when that hijacking occurred?"

"Well . . . yes." Ramón shrugged again, but she noticed that his fingers tightened over the earring. "You can see why I have an interest."

Yes, I can, Nancy thought. An anthropologist who thinks Margaret Mead went to Tahiti instead of Samoa, an experienced sailor who doesn't know who won the America's Cup race, a man who "by chance" happened to be in the same area each time the pirates attacked. And a man who still owned, and once wore, a gold earring just like the one the pirates had given Joe Mason!

Yes, Ramón DaSilvio, Nancy said to herself, I certainly *can* understand why you're interested. And now *I'm* very interested in *you*.

Chapter

Four

"LEE PO," BECCA CALLED in her soft southern accent. "It's about time to head on back."

The captain said nothing, but Nancy noticed that he gripped the wheel so tightly his knuckles turned white as he altered course. Why did he react so strongly to a simple order from his boss?

During the short return trip, Nancy tried to catch another glimpse of Ramón's earring, but he kept it concealed in his hand. When they pulled up to the pier, he put it back in his pants pocket.

The men helped Lee Po with the docking lines, and Nancy found a chance to talk to Becca alone.

"Becca," Nancy said. "I'm curious about your friend Ramón. Where did you meet him?"

"Let's see," she said. "I think it was in the Virgin Islands. Yes, at a party in Charlotte

Amalie. Then I ran into him again in St. Kitts. In fact, he's the one who told me about Belize, and that's why I'm here."

"Really?" Nancy said. "That's interesting."

"He's terribly handsome, don't you think?" Becca giggled. "These Latin men are so romantic. I just love them."

Nancy smiled, thinking that Becca obviously loved all men without regard to nationality, creed, or color.

Chang, the young boy, signaled to Becca from the cabin doorway. "Excuse me," Becca said, and went over to him. She smiled and nodded at Chang's whispered question. He grinned and went back into the cabin. Nancy wondered why he wasn't in school and where his parents were. Lee Po wasn't old enough to be his father, but perhaps they were brothers or cousins.

"Becca," David said when they were ready to leave. "I'm giving a pool party tomorrow at Casa Playa, and I'm hoping you'll be able to come."

"Why, I'd just *love* to," Becca said.

"Great," David said. "I'll ask Jerry to pick you up about noon and drive you out to our place." He turned to the anthropologist. "Ramón, I'd be honored if you came, too."

"Thank you, but I have a research trip planned. I must get on with my work," Ramón said.

He stood next to Becca on the deck waving goodbye as Nancy, Ned, and David drove away.

"David," Nancy asked, "could we stop by the library on the way home? I'd like to check past issues of the newspapers to see if I can find out more about the pirates." She didn't mention that she also wanted to double-check a few facts about Margaret Mead and perhaps find a picture or description of the other earrings left by the pirates. Until she was sure she had reason to doubt Ramón, she'd keep her suspicions to herself.

"Pirates!" David said. "I'd almost forgotten about them."

Ned gently squeezed Nancy's shoulder. "You don't know our Nan. Once she becomes curious about a mystery, she has to find the answer."

"I'm sure the Coast Guard will solve the case," Nancy said. "But I can't help wondering about the pirates' strange behavior, especially the ear-piercing. It's just so odd!"

At the library, while Ned and David were locating back issues of newspapers, Nancy checked with the reference librarian, who helped her confirm the fact that Margaret Mead had indeed gone to Samoa and had not done any studies of the people of Tahiti.

When she rejoined Ned and David, they had already located an article on the first hijacking. Slowly the three of them scrolled through the newspaper accounts, which had been preserved on microfilm.

Nancy stopped at a photo of one of the rescued

victims. The picture was fuzzy, but from what she could see, the earring in the man's ear looked a lot like Ramón's simple circle of gold. Though she realized Ramón's earring didn't necessarily link him to the piracies, she decided she'd have another talk with the Cuban.

They continued to scroll through the microfilmed newspaper articles.

"Look at this," Nancy said, pointing to a paragraph describing the rescue of the victims of the third hijacking. "This is strange. The life raft drifted for a week and was found when an anonymous caller suggested the searchers try an area almost twenty miles from where they'd been looking."

"But how did the caller know where the raft was?" David asked.

"The homing device!" Nancy quickly scanned the rest of the article. "Yes, they found a transmitter on that raft, too, and just like Cutler, the owner had never seen it before."

Ned frowned. "But that means the pirates were the ones tracking the raft."

"That's right," Nancy said. "The anonymous caller had to be one of the pirates." She looked at them. "But why would they bother to phone in a tip?"

"That is really strange," David said.

"I agree," Nancy said. "I'm getting more and more curious about these people. There has to be an explanation for their behavior."

Ned grinned. "You've got that look in your eye, Nan. Get ready, David, I think we're about to become involved in another detective case."

Nancy smiled. "Well, I might ask just a few questions here and there . . ."

Ned laughed and hugged her. "That's my Nancy!"

That evening they dined at Casa Playa with David's parents, Robert Cutler, Joe Mason, and David's friend, Manny Mai. Nancy was glad to see the handsome, cheerful Mayan again.

Mrs. Peck had returned from Placentia in the afternoon. She was an attractive woman, with pale blond hair like her son's, and she spoke with a slight British accent. She told Nancy she'd met her husband in London and still went home every year during Belize's rainy season.

"When I say rain," Mrs. Peck said as Marie passed a platter of spiced beef, "I don't mean a mist or a drizzle. It's a torrential downpour, with buckets of water falling in solid sheets. And the insects! Hundreds of thousands of them hatch each minute."

"Now, Adrienne, you mustn't exaggerate," Kevin Peck chided. "You know you love this country."

"Yes, I do," his wife admitted. "Even if I'm not too fond of bugs. It's exciting to live here and help make decisions that will affect Belize's future."

"My mother," David explained to their guests,

"works with several organizations that have helped set aside nature reserves, such as the baboon sanctuary, Mountain Pine Ridge, the Cockscomb Basin Wildlife Sanctuary . . ."

"And we're going to protect many more areas," Mrs. Peck put in. "You might say my husband and I represent opposing interests. I'm trying to conserve our reef and wildlife, while he's trying to develop various industries such as tourism."

"People need to eat, Adrienne," Kevin Peck said. "Belize has always been very poor," he told his guests. "If tourists come to see all our natural beauty, it will create jobs and also bring in money."

"That seems like a good combination to me," Robert Cutler said. "You can protect the land and earn dollars at the same time."

"It's more complicated than that in practice," David said. "For instance, if we now have twenty snorkelers a day at Hol Chan, and then suddenly there are two hundred, more boats will be required. Boats bring in pollution and their anchors will disturb the bottom where many creatures breed and live. Soon the fragile reef will be damaged."

"Yes," Mrs. Peck agreed. "As just one example, if you touch a piece of coral, you remove the coating that protects the tiny animals that make up the coral and they die."

"Here's another example," Manny said. "Parrot fish are delicious to eat, but tourists love to see them. They're beautiful, so Belize recently passed laws to protect them for the scuba divers and the snorkelers. The problem is," Manny continued, "that for all those long miles of the reef, we are preserving only one tiny part of the system, the parrot fish. And parrot fish eat coral. If you have too many of them nibbling away, you end up with a dead reef."

"I see," Nancy said. "By protecting only one species, one part of the community, you throw off the natural balance."

"But if we didn't protect the parrot fish," David said, "we'd become like some of the Caribbean islands, where you can swim for hours and not see a single one."

"Why not protect all the species of fish along the reef?" Ned asked.

"Fishing is a major industry in Belize," David's father answered. "It would not only be foolish, it would be impossible to make the entire reef off limits."

Nancy said, "It seems like a complicated issue. How do you solve the problem?"

"Very carefully," David's parents said at the same time. They looked at each other and laughed.

David smiled at them. "We deal with these issues and many, many more every day. It's hard to find the right balance. I'm only glad I live in a country that cares equally about both its natural beauty and its people."

After dinner they discussed plans for the pool

party David was giving the next day. Robert Cutler and Joe Mason went up to bed early, still tired from their three days on the raft, and the others soon followed.

Nancy tossed and turned in bed. Aside from the complex issues they'd discussed at dinner, and her suspicions of Ramón, she kept wondering about the very polite pirates. Why did they track the rafts? Why did they tell the searchers where to locate the victims? And why did they pierce the men's ears?

She finally drifted off and dreamed of masked men wearing gold earrings, swarming over the reef capturing parrot fish, but suddenly there was a lot of noise and confusion, banging sounds and loud voices.

She awoke and realized it was morning but the noises hadn't stopped. Doors slammed, people shouted, phones rang. She threw on a robe and went out into the hall just as Joe Mason hurried past her door.

"Mr. Mason, what's wrong?" she asked.

"Rob's disappeared," he said. "I think he's been kidnapped!"

Chapter
Five

"Mr. Cutler? Kidnapped?" Nancy gasped. "Are you sure?"

"Yes!" Mason replied. "When I went to get him for our early morning jog he was gone. His bed is torn apart, and he's not anywhere in the house. We're about to search the grounds right now."

"I'll get dressed." Nancy closed the door and quickly pulled on white shorts and a blue T-shirt, then hurried downstairs.

Mrs. Peck was on the phone in the living room, talking to the police. Outside, Nancy could see David, Mr. Peck, Joe Mason, and Ned inspecting the gardens and outbuildings.

"Are they quite sure Mr. Cutler isn't in the house?" Nancy asked as Mrs. Peck hung up the phone.

"We've checked everywhere," Mrs. Peck answered with a sigh. "The police are on the way."

"Could I look at Mr. Cutler's room?" Nancy asked.

"Of course, but be careful not to touch anything," Mrs. Peck said. "My husband insisted that we not disturb possible clues."

"That was wise," Nancy said.

The phone rang again. "Marie, would you take Ms. Drew up, please?" Mrs. Peck lifted the receiver. "Hello? Yes, Governor, I'm afraid it's true . . . not a sign of him."

Nancy followed the housekeeper upstairs to a room at the far end of the hall. The yellow bedsheets were strewn across the floor, as if Cutler had dragged them to the French doors that stood wide open and led to the veranda. The bed was bare. Where was the pillow? Nancy wondered.

She checked the closets and drawers: no pillow. Cutler's clothes, recently bought in Belize City, were neatly hung up. His razor and toothbrush were in the bathroom medicine cabinet, and a cotton robe hung on the back of the door.

"If he left on his own," Nancy said, "he obviously planned to be back soon."

"Maybe he went for a walk in the night," Marie suggested.

"It's possible, but why are the sheets off the bed?" Nancy glanced around the room and noticed that none of the lamps were on. "And why not turn on a light to keep from stumbling in the dark?"

Nancy stepped out onto the veranda, careful not to disturb anything. An image formed in her mind: Cutler being dragged from bed, clutching the only thing he could grab, the sheets. "I wonder if the pillow was held over his mouth to keep him from shouting for help," Nancy mused.

She walked along the veranda to the stairs leading down to the garden. From there she could see the driveway and the long dirt lane that led across the flat savanna to the main road.

"If anyone asks, please tell them I'll be right back," she called to Marie. She hurried down the steps. The lane was the only access to the house. If Cutler had been kidnapped, his captors would have had to come by car, Nancy figured, but they probably wouldn't have dared park too close to the house. It was likely they had dragged—or carried—Cutler down the lane, possibly as far as the main road.

Nancy searched for footprints in the dirt road but saw nothing on the dry, rocky soil. As she neared the main road she caught a glimpse of yellow under a palmetto palm. She ran over and saw it was a pillow; its case matched the yellow sheets in Cutler's room.

Sirens wailed in the distance, then drew nearer. One police car stopped at Nancy's signal while the other two continued on to the house. The stern-faced sergeant who had accepted the homing transmitter from her after the rescue emerged from the car.

"Sergeant—" Nancy glanced at the name on his uniform—"Cordova. I'm Nancy Drew, and we met a couple of days ago—"

"I remember," the sergeant interrupted, frowning. "What can I do for you?"

Nancy explained her theory about the way Cutler might have been abducted, then pointed to the pillow. "They probably threw it away after they hustled Cutler into the car. They wouldn't have needed it any longer."

Cordova glanced at the house in the distance, then gave Nancy a sharp look. "Interesting, Ms. Drew, but I suggest you leave the investigation to us. We're the professionals."

"I've had some detective experience back in the States," Nancy said, "and I thought perhaps—"

"I'll send someone out for the pillow," Cordova said abruptly. "Would you like a ride back to the house?"

"Yes, thank you." Nancy got into his car, thinking of the warm welcome she'd received from the many Belizeans she'd met. Why did she have to stumble across the only man in the country who apparently didn't know how to smile?

At Casa Playa, the police had taken full charge of the investigation. Nancy found Ned and David in the breakfast room, eating pancakes. She accepted a cup of coffee and told them about finding the pillow.

"Your theory makes perfect sense," Ned said. Nancy smiled. "Just don't say that to Sergeant Cordova. The question is, who are the kidnappers? They must have known that Cutler was staying here."

"That should narrow the search a bit," David said. "But Belize is such a small country, there are probably very few people who *don't* know."

"He's right, Nan," Ned said. "I was amazed to learn the population is only about 240,000. Some of our small cities have more people than that."

"Besides," David added, "the rescue was front-page news, and at least one article mentioned that my father had invited Cutler and Mason to stay here."

"The usual reason for kidnapping is to collect ransom," Nancy said. "I wonder if that's why Cutler was taken. Has anyone found a note demanding money?"

David shook his head. "Not yet."

"Maybe they'll deliver it or call soon," Nancy said.

"Why do you sound doubtful?" Ned asked.

Nancy took a sip of coffee. "Within a few days we've had two major crimes, kidnapping and piracy. And in both cases Robert Cutler was the victim. Is that only a coincidence, or are the two crimes related?"

"It *is* odd," David said. "The pirates had Cutler and they turned him loose. Why would they change their minds and take him back?"

"I don't know," Nancy said. "But thanks to the homing device, they know he made it to shore, and as you pointed out, David, it's no secret that he was staying here with your family."

"It sounds as though you think the pirates are the kidnappers," David said.

"Unless we get a ransom note that leads us to another person or persons, it's logical to think the same group came back for him," Nancy explained. "Maybe the pirates found something on the *Windchime* that gave them a reason to need him again. Perhaps he knows the combination to a safe they can't crack, or the secret code to get into a bank account."

"That makes sense, Nancy," David said.

"If I'm right, my theory is good news in a way. It means that, as of last night at least, the pirates were still in Belize and not out somewhere at sea."

"But will they stay in the area now that they have Cutler?" Ned asked.

"If they don't, there's a good chance they might be spotted. The Coast Guard has broadcast a description of the *Windchime* as well as the other missing yachts. Every boat in the Caribbean will be on the lookout for them."

She poured herself another cup of coffee. "I'll admit," she went on, "that even if the kidnappers are still in Belize, I've got few clues to go on, and the kidnappers could be anywhere in the country. Nevertheless, I might as well follow what leads I have and see where they take me. Right now there's one person I'd like to talk to again." She told them her suspicions about Ramón.

"Ramón?" Ned said, surprised. "I'm sure he's a real anthropologist. When he said Tahiti instead of Samoa, it must have been a slip of the tongue."

David jumped to Ramón's defense, too. "And just because he has a gold earring doesn't mean he's connected with the pirates. Lots of guys wear them these days, and the one you describe is a very common style."

"But it won't hurt to talk to him," Nancy said. "David, may I borrow your phone? Ramón said he was staying at the Sunrise Hotel."

"Sure, I'll place the call for you." David glanced at his watch. "Oh, boy, it's after nine. My friends will be arriving in less than three hours. Maybe I should cancel the party."

Nancy had seen the caterer's van unloading trays of food at the kitchen door when she was driven back to the house by Sergeant Cordova. "Why don't you check with the police?" she asked. "Everything is ready for the party, and unless they object, why not go ahead with it?"

"Good idea." David dialed the hotel, then gave the telephone to Nancy while he went to find the police commissioner. The desk clerk had a thick Creole accent, but finally he made it clear to Nancy that Ramón had checked out.

"Do you know where he went?" Nancy asked.

"He ask about buses to San Ignacio, in the mountains near the border of Guatemala, and hotels. I tell him, stay at El Tucán. It's good— very clean," the clerk offered.

When Nancy hung up she said to Ned, "I don't like it. Mr. Cutler disappears and Ramón takes off for San Ignacio—*if* that's where he went. I know he said he had more research to do, but he could be laying down a false trail."

"If he does go to San Ignacio," David offered as he came back into the room, "we can drive out there later this afternoon. My family has a lodge in the area, Casa Maya, and we could stay overnight."

"What about your party?" Nancy asked. "Will you still have it?"

"The police will be done here before noon, and my parents say I may as well go ahead. Canceling it won't help find Mr. Cutler, wherever he is."

"I wonder if there's something in Robert Cutler's background that might give us a clue to either the piracy or the kidnapping, or both," Nancy put in. "May I use your phone again, David? I'd like to call my father and ask him to check into Cutler's past. He can find out about Ramón at the same time."

"Sure." David dialed the international number, and Nancy spoke with her father, Carson Drew. She assured him she was having a good time and told him that while she wasn't officially investigating a case, she needed a little information. He promised to help but jokingly scolded her for getting involved in another mystery when she was supposed to be on vacation.

Nancy was smiling when she hung up, but then she became serious. "I think we should talk to Joe Mason. Maybe he can tell us something about his friend Robert Cutler."

"I saw Mr. Mason out on the patio," David said. "I'll get him."

Joe Mason was frowning when he and David came into the breakfast room. "Poor Rob," he said, accepting a cup of coffee from Nancy. "He must be furious at whoever took him. He's used to having things his own way and won't react well to this at all."

"Why do you say that?" Nancy asked.

"Rob is very wealthy," Joe said. "He's a banker, and he's made a number of clever investments that have let him live very comfortably. That's how he was able to take three months off for this Caribbean cruise."

"Do you know him well?" Nancy asked.

"Not really. I met him through business, and we hit it off. When he found out that I like to sail, he invited me to join him for a week down here. My wife wasn't too happy about it, but Rob insisted she had nothing to worry about." He smiled wryly. "I should have listened to Beth."

"I gather Mr. Cutler is not married," Nancy said.

"No, he's single—probably the most eligible bachelor in Miami. He hinted once that he'd been married a long time ago but didn't like it much. I think the problem is that he enjoys boats and the freedom it gives him."

"Can you think of any reason why he might have been kidnapped?" Nancy asked.

Joe Mason shrugged. "Probably for money. What else could it be?"

"We'll find out when—or if—we get a ransom demand," Nancy said. "Thanks, Mr. Mason. If you think of anything else that might be helpful, would you let me know?"

"Sure will." He left the room, shaking his head and muttering, "Poor Rob."

By twelve-thirty the gardens at Casa Playa were filled with young people. They swam in the pool and danced under the palms while rock music thumped from loudspeakers. Nancy stood on the lower veranda beside a bougainvillea bush loaded with scarlet blossoms, thinking the festive scene was a big contrast to the grim search for Robert Cutler earlier that morning.

"Nancy!" Manny Mai appeared and gave her a playful hug. He was wearing a shirt splotched with huge orange and purple flowers. Nancy thought the wild print looked great on him.

"Why so serious?" he asked. "Come join the party."

"I'm waiting to make a phone call." She smiled at his handsome face with the sparkling dark eyes and cheerful grin. "I'll be with you in a moment."

"Hurry, I'm saving my first dance for you." Manny winked at her and headed for the barbecue pit, where chicken and steak sizzled over hot coals.

Nancy checked her watch. She figured Ramón must have reached San Ignacio by now. She went inside to phone El Tucán. "Yes," the hotel clerk reported after she'd dialed the number. "Mr. DaSilvio, he check in, but then he go out."

"Thank you," Nancy said, and hung up. She felt her impatience growing. She wanted to leave for San Ignacio immediately, but she knew she'd have to wait until the party ended at three. She was relieved at least that Ramón had actually gone to the mountains and she knew where to find him.

As Nancy headed toward the pool, she saw Becca hand Ned a tall glass of lime juice. Becca was wearing a peekaboo cover-up over a tiny lavender bikini that showed off her shapely figure. From the admiring glance Ned gave her, it was clear that he appreciated it.

"Nancy, you're free at last," Manny said, sweeping her into his arms. "Dance with me."

Nancy tore her gaze away from Ned and Becca and tried to return Manny's enthusiastic smile. The band was playing "Yellow Bird," and she moved in the time to the bouncy calypso beat. Out of the corner of her eye, she saw Jerry approach Ned and the heiress. A minute later Jerry whisked Becca away toward the band, and

Ned wandered off, joining a crowd surrounding David.

Nancy began to relax and enjoy herself.

Manny was a wonderful dancer. His smooth, muscular body moved easily to the beat, and his eyes glowed with pleasure. "Ah, how lucky I am," he said, "to be dancing with such a beautiful girl on such a beautiful day!"

Nancy's silky pink cover-up concealed her white bikini but clung to her as she danced. She couldn't help noticing that Manny seemed to approve of her slender curves. "You don't have to work today?" she asked.

"When my friend David gives a party, I always take time off. Work is important, but so is play." Manny spun her around, then expertly caught her in his strong arms. Nancy laughed out loud with delight, and then she heard applause. Several couples had stopped dancing to watch the two of them.

They danced to several numbers, then cooled off in the pool. When Nancy toweled herself dry she spotted Ned and Becca, alone again in a corner of the garden, so she accepted Manny's invitation to join him during lunch.

They found a table under a red mangrove tree, and while they ate he told her about growing up in a large family. Although his parents were poor, they'd managed to send him to a good school where he'd met David. In spite of their very different backgrounds, he and David soon discovered they had many interests in common and the two had been close friends ever since.

Manny also talked about his boat and his life on the water. Nancy found herself liking him more and more, and not just because of his good looks and cheerful nature. He was very bright and cared passionately about the coral reef and all of Belize's natural treasures.

"Hi," Becca said, approaching them with a plate of food. Ned and David were behind her. "Mind if we join you?"

"Please do." Manny jumped up and pulled extra chairs over to the table.

"David just told me the most exciting thing, Nancy," Becca said as the three of them sat down. "He said you're a detective. Why, I had no idea!"

"Well, I've had experience with a few cases," Nancy admitted. "But I'm on vacation now."

Becca, grinning, wagged her finger at her. "Now, don't you be so modest. David said you're investigating those horrible ol' pirates and poor Mr. Cutler's kidnapping, too. Why, I think that's just so *thrilling.*"

"It's nothing official—" Nancy protested.

Becca interrupted her. "And you're driving out west this very afternoon to question a suspect. May I come along, too? I've never seen a suspect grilled. Besides, I hear there's a lot of land out there my daddy might want to invest in."

"Um, sure," Nancy said. She wasn't sure how

Becca would react when she found out the person she was planning to question was Ramón.

A few minutes later Nancy went to get dessert. She had just chosen a chocolate éclair when she overheard a chilling conversation.

The dessert table stood in front of a cluster of palms. The voices came from behind the trees and she couldn't see the speakers. "I don't care what you say," a male voice said. "Manny Mai's asking for trouble."

"Just because he takes his boat out late at night?" a girl replied. "That doesn't prove he's doing anything illegal."

"I saw him several times, and he sneaks out of the harbor, trying not to attract attention. He's always alone, so he's not taking out a night fishing party. He keeps looking over his shoulder to see if he's being followed, and then, when he thinks he can't be spotted, he guns the engine and disappears into the dark. I'm telling you, Manny Mai's up to no good!"

Nancy felt goose bumps wash over her. Manny —handsome, laughing, cheerful Manny—acting so suspiciously. What could he possibly be doing on the ocean late at night? she wondered. He wasn't . . . no, he couldn't be involved with the pirates, could he?

Chapter
Six

Nancy, very upset, said nothing to the others about the conversation she'd overheard. When Manny announced he had to get back to Ambergris Cay, Nancy didn't try to question him. She needed time to think before she talked to him again.

After the other party guests left, Nancy noticed Manny's orange and purple shirt on the back of a chair where he'd tossed it before they went swimming. She took it upstairs with her, planning to return it as soon as she saw him again.

Once in her room, she hung the shirt in the closet, then began to pack for her overnight stay in the mountains. She put a few clothes in a small bag, her mind still on Manny.

There probably is a perfectly good reason that

he takes his boat out at night, Nancy told herself. How could someone so lively and charming be guilty of piracy or kidnapping? But she knew from experience that villains could be quite likable people.

She also knew she had to put her personal feelings aside, but with Manny it was difficult. Face it, Nan, she admitted, you don't simply like him, you *really* like him. And if it weren't for Ned . . .

Ned! His fascination with Becca was beginning to annoy Nancy. Although Becca had done nothing to encourage him, she did seem to enjoy his attention.

Nancy reached into the closet for her favorite blue dress, and her hand brushed against Manny's shirt. Something stiff crinkled in the pocket. She realized she'd noticed it before, but now she wondered if Manny had left important papers behind. She pulled out the sheet of notepaper and read the few lines in bold block printing with many words crossed out:

". . . the danger is serious . . . this is not a joke . . . can't wait any longer . . . act now or I will have to . . ."

Nancy held the paper up to the light but couldn't make out the missing words, which were heavily scribbled over. The conclusion was clear, however: this was a rough draft of a threatening letter.

Her heart pounding, Nancy slipped the paper

into her purse. Oh, Manny, she thought, what are you doing? Who are you writing to? This sounds a lot like a ransom note. . . .

"Ready to go, Nancy?" David called as he went down the hallway. "We should get started."

"Coming!" Nancy hastily packed the blue dress, zipped the bag, and hurried downstairs.

David helped Nancy into the front seat of a dark green Jeep. "Wait until you see the mountain roads," he said, grinning. "Some of the potholes could swallow up my little sports car."

Ned appeared with Becca, and they climbed into the backseat. Soon they were off.

After stopping at *La Moola* so that Becca could pick up a change of clothes, they set off on the drive to San Ignacio. The paved, two-lane highway led almost directly west, crossing the flat plains with its low bushes and patches of mangrove swamps. It was very hot.

Nancy tried to distract herself from worrying about Manny by concentrating on the scenery.

"What's that?" she asked, noticing a raised mound beside the road. It was shaped like a flat-topped pyramid, about twenty feet high, and covered with grass. Cows were grazing on it.

"It's a Mayan ruin," David said. "There are thousands of them all over Belize, and only a fraction of the sites have been excavated."

"It's downright odd to see cows standing on what used to be a house or a temple," Becca said.

"We're now in the Cayo district," David explained. "You'll see lots of ranches and farms.

Becca, this is one area your father might want to invest in. . . ."

Nancy tuned out David and Becca's discussion. Her thoughts kept drifting back to Manny and that terrible note. The strong, heavy handwriting made the words even more ominous: the danger is serious . . . not a joke . . . act now or I will . . . What will you do, Manny? she wondered.

Nancy gave herself a little shake. Until you talk to Manny, you won't get the answers, she told herself, so there's nothing you can do right now.

Nancy forced her thoughts away from Manny and thought about what she would ask Ramón when they found him. Was he involved with the pirates and/or Cutler's kidnapping? She had to admit her suspicions were based on weak evidence, but her instincts told her he wasn't exactly the person he claimed to be. What was he covering up?

After an hour's drive across the plains the rounded humps of the Maya Mountains appeared in the distance. As they climbed higher the air began to grow cooler. Finally, they crossed a shallow river and drove into the small town of San Ignacio.

David stopped in front of El Tucán Inn. "Ramón sure has modest taste when it comes to hotels," he commented. "Both the Sunrise in Belize City and this place have definitely seen better days."

Nancy went into the dark, ramshackle lobby and asked for Ramón.

"He not come back yet," the desk clerk said. "Maybe pretty soon."

"Do you know where he went?" Nancy said.

"He take taxi, go to Xunantunich."

"Shune-an-tu-*nich*," Nancy said, trying to repeat the name correctly. "Thanks." She went back to the car. "David, do you know where Xunantunich is?"

"Sure." David started up the motor. "It's the Mayan temple a few miles out of town. Is Ramón there?"

"I hope so," Nancy said.

"Wait a minute," Becca said. "Do you mean to say my friend *Ramón* is the suspect you want to question? David never did say who y'all wanted to talk to. Why, that's just plain silly! Ramón's no pirate."

"I didn't say he was," Nancy replied. "I just wanted to discuss a theory with him. It's about Margaret Mead, the anthropologist."

"Oh, well, that's different." Becca sat back and pouted. "But I have to tell you, I'm downright disappointed. I thought we were going to grill a dangerous criminal."

Nancy smiled. "Sorry, Becca. Not all detective work is as exciting as you might think."

They took the highway that ran beside the Mopan River, where women knelt on the banks washing clothes. Soon David turned off toward a small hand-cranked cable ferry and drove the

Jeep aboard. The trip across the pretty, tree-shaded river took only moments.

"Now for the real challenge," David said as they started up a steep, narrow dirt road, deeply rutted with giant potholes. The Jeep groaned and shuddered, but at last they reached a parking area shaded by the tallest palm trees Nancy had ever seen.

They walked up a short path, and as they came around a bend, Nancy gasped in amazement. "This is absolutely awesome!"

The towering ruins of the Mayan temple rose up in tiers before her, the ancient slabs of rock forming a castle in the sky. An enormous pyramid was the base, with grassy terraced levels leading up to bare rock carved with Mayan symbols.

"I see Ramón!" Becca pointed to a small figure on the topmost platform.

Nancy led the group past an archaeologist directing a work crew and up stone steps to the first terraced level and followed a path that circled around to the back. Then they began to climb.

To reach the uppermost level, they had to use a shaky metal ladder. Nancy went first, and as her head reached the top she saw Ramón standing on a small stone terrace, lost in thought. Low rock walls encased two sides of the narrow space and a small chamber was visible behind him, but there was no railing across the front to guard against a fall.

Ramón started with surprise when he spotted her. "Ms. Drew! What are you doing here?"

Nancy grinned as she scrambled onto the platform. "We thought we'd drop by and say hi. You didn't see us coming?"

Ramón frowned. "I was . . . contemplating the mysteries of the Mayans."

Ned and David stepped off the ladder, followed by Becca. Becca stood up, took one look at the open platform and the vast rolling countryside far below, and moaned. She began to sway, clearly dizzy.

"Sit down, Becca," Ned said. "Let me help you." He pulled her back to the entryway of the tiny chamber.

"What is it?" Nancy asked. "Fear of heights?"

"Yes!" Becca gasped, her breath shallow and ragged, her face ashen. "It . . . just . . . hit . . . me . . . so . . . suddenly. Oooohhhhh."

Nancy gazed out at the countryside. She knew the fear of falling was a strong element in vertigo. It could strike suddenly, leaving the victim with a sickening, queasy feeling. "She's got to go down right away. It's the only cure," Nancy urged.

"I'll take her," Ned said quickly.

But it took both him and David to ease Becca down the wobbly ladder. She clung to each rung, petrified, barely able to move. At last they got her to the lower level and helped her stagger down to the ground.

Ramón watched them as they circled around the ruins and disappeared from sight. "Poor

Becca. It must be an absolutely miserable feeling."

"She wasn't bothered at all on the lower levels," Nancy said. "But up here, there's an eerie, almost mystical, feeling, isn't there?"

He nodded. "This was a very important temple. Perhaps it was the home of a king. Almost certainly it was the site of religious ceremonies."

"The Mayans sometimes made human sacrifices, didn't they?" Nancy asked.

"Most scholars think so, at least near the end of the Classic period," he said. "It's quite possible that some unlucky slaves ended their time on earth right here on the very spot where we are standing."

Nancy shuddered. "I'm glad the Mayans gave that up ages ago." She thought briefly of Manny, then turned to Ramón. "Xunantunich is fascinating, but I really came to see you."

"Me? Why, I'm most flattered." Ramón slicked his dark hair back from his forehead.

"Did you know Robert Cutler has disappeared?" Nancy asked.

"Cutler?" he said, surprised. "Isn't he one of the men you rescued from the raft?"

"Yes," Nancy said. "Do you know anything about it?" She watched closely for his reaction.

Ramón seemed genuinely puzzled. "Why do you ask me? I've never met the man."

"I thought you might have run into him, since you've both been traveling around the Caribbean." Nancy noticed that Ramón had removed the gold earring from his pocket and was toying with it again. "That looks like a valuable piece of jewelry," she added.

"What? This?" Ramón glanced at the simple gold circle as if surprised to see it, then quickly stuffed it back in his pocket. "It's not so valuable, except for sentimental reasons. Someone gave it to me, a girl I very much cared about, but that was a long time ago."

"Did you ever wear it?" Nancy asked.

"Yes, but not now. It is perhaps a little undignified for a respected anthropologist to have a ring in his ear."

Nancy thought a moment and decided to gamble. "Ramón, may I be frank? Yesterday you mentioned Margaret Mead's study of Tahiti, but you made a mistake. Mead went to Samoa. If you're an anthropologist, as you claim, you would have known that."

"But—but, I am, I assure you!" He wiped sudden beads of sweat off his brow.

"Where did you go to college?" Nancy asked.

"NYU! New York University!" He took a step toward her. They were both standing near the front edge of the platform now.

"NYU?" Nancy casually took a couple of steps back toward the safety of the stone walls. "Do you know Professor Sisson? She's a friend of my father, and she teaches in the anthropology department."

"Um, y-y-yes, of course . . . but—but not well . . ." he stammered.

It was clear to Nancy he was lying. "Describe her to me."

Ramón walked toward her, his shoulders stiff. He stopped and bowed his head, then sighed and held out his hands, as if begging for mercy.

"All right," he said quietly, "I do not yet have my degree. I am teaching myself as I perform the work I love. When I complete my paper, if I write it well, perhaps NYU will read it and accept me in their program."

"Why do you pass yourself off as an anthropologist?" Nancy asked.

"Without a degree, I cannot get people to talk to me, give me the information I need. Try to understand, please, Ms. Drew." He began to pace, nervously smoothing his hair back. "I have always hungered for an education, but I come from a poor fishing village. When I was twelve, my father asked me to work on his boat to help feed the family."

"But you dress well now," Nancy observed. "You seem to have money."

He gave her a bashful smile. "My grandmother knew how I yearned for school. When she died, she left me all she had saved. It wasn't much, but enough to buy clothes and pay a seaman to smuggle me out of Cuba aboard his cargo ship. Since then, I have relied on the kindness of many people such as Becca, who became friends and offered me food, sometimes a bed for a day or two. I take jobs as a crew member on boats now and then. I manage. My work is all-important."

Nancy was moved by his story. Ramón seemed utterly sincere, and she recognized the deep need in his voice. Almost ashamed of her suspicions, she walked toward the front of the platform, gazing at the magnificent countryside spread out below her.

"Please, Ms. Drew, you are the only one who knows my secret," he said from behind her. "You will guard it well?"

"Of course," she began to say when suddenly she felt a hand on her shoulder, pushing her. She staggered forward, to the very edge of the platform, and her foot slid over into space!

Chapter

Seven

NANCY FLUNG HER ARMS OUT, trying to regain her balance as she teetered on one foot. Suddenly something grabbed her wrist. She felt a tremendous jerk, and she was flung backward. She landed on the platform and rolled up against the stone wall.

"Ms. Drew! Are you all right?" Ramón bent over her, his dark eyes full of fear.

She sat up, rubbing her wrist. It ached slightly, but she knew Ramón's strong grip had saved her. "I'm fine. What happened?"

"It was all my fault!" Ramón cried. "How can I be so clumsy? I meant only to touch you, to thank you for your understanding." He put his hands to his face and shook his head. "I'm such a fool."

"It's all right," Nancy said. "It was an accident." She recalled the feeling, a heavy hand on her shoulder, and realized it had felt like a push because Ramón was moving quickly toward her. Her own startled reaction had helped throw her off balance. "I'm okay, but I think it's time to go, don't you?"

"Yes, yes. Can you ever forgive me?"

Ramón continued to apologize all the way down. Just before they joined the others waiting by the van, Nancy said, "Ramón, I understand and I don't blame you. It was an accident." She found his emotional display a bit draining. "Let's forget it. There's no need to mention it again."

Humbly Ramón agreed, and Nancy, relieved, greeted her friends with cheery hellos. Becca was fully recovered from her attack of vertigo and had both David and Ned laughing at a story about a man she had met in the Virgin Islands.

Nancy took David aside. "I don't think Ramón is involved in either Cutler's kidnapping or the piracy," she told him. "Could we invite him to stay with us at Casa Maya? He doesn't have much money, and I hate to think of him alone in that hotel."

"Sure," David said. "He can stay as long as he likes. There's plenty of room, and the staff is always ready for guests."

They stopped at El Tucán Inn while Ramón checked out, then drove to Casa Maya, a spacious and airy lodge spread out over a hillside. Dinner was ready and they ate on the patio, watching hummingbirds fly among the flowers.

After dessert, both Becca and Ramón, tired from the long day, decided to go to bed early, leaving Nancy, Ned, and David to linger over their coffee.

"Why did you change your mind about Ramón, Nancy?" David asked. "What did you find out?"

"I can't tell you, David," Nancy said. "I'm sorry, but Ramón made me promise to keep our talk confidential. In any case, we can eliminate him as a suspect."

"Then that leaves us with *no* suspects," Ned said.

"Not quite," Nancy said slowly. "I'm not sure how to tell you . . ." She looked at David, Manny Mai's best friend. "I overheard a conversation at your pool party that disturbed me." She told them about Manny sneaking out of the harbor at night and then, very reluctantly, showed them the note she'd found in his shirt pocket.

"That's Manny's handwriting," David muttered. "But this note says so little, it could mean anything."

Nancy could see that David was unhappy that she suspected his best friend and decided not to press the issue. "You're probably right," she said gently.

David didn't seem to hear her. "Manny couldn't possibly be involved with pirates or a kidnapping. That's a ridiculous idea."

"I agree," Nancy said. "I find it hard to believe, too, but—"

"I'll bet you do," Ned interrupted. "I saw you and Manny at the party. You were having a *very* good time together."

Nancy was astonished at Ned's outburst. Then she became angry. "I'm surprised you bothered to notice. You couldn't keep your eyes off Becca."

"I noticed all right," Ned said. "I'd have to be blind not to see the way Manny looks at you. He—"

"Hey, you two," David said. "Take it easy. We're all friends here. Nancy, you know Becca flirts with all the guys. She isn't playing favorites with Ned. And, Ned, half the girls in Belize are in love with Manny. That's the way he is. He's not seriously trying to take Nancy away from you."

Nancy bit her lip. She was sorry this was happening in front of David. If she and Ned were going to fight, it should be in private. She had to push her emotions aside and return to the case.

She forced herself to smile at David. "You're right. Tell me more about Manny. Why are you so sure he's not doing anything wrong?"

David relaxed. "I didn't say he wouldn't do *anything* wrong, only that he wouldn't get involved in a serious crime. Manny is rather a maverick. He has strong beliefs, and if society doesn't always agree, he doesn't care."

"What do you mean?" Nancy asked.

"Well, there was the case of the jaguar poachers last year. Our jaguars are protected as an endangered species, but we don't have enough people to patrol everywhere. Manny found out a gang of poachers was taking babies from the wildlife sanctuary, and he reported it to the authorities. When they didn't act fast enough, Manny went after them alone."

"What happened?" Ned asked.

"The poachers returned to their truck one night with two jaguar kittens and found the tires slashed, the engine ripped apart, and Manny waiting with a gun. He forced the poachers to return the kittens to their mother, then turned the poachers in to the police. He got in big trouble for taking the law into his own hands, but at least the gang was arrested."

"He could have been killed," Nancy said.

"Not our Manny," David said. "He was born with an angel sitting on his shoulder."

Nancy wasn't ready to assume that Manny was as innocent as David thought, but she decided to drop the subject for the moment. "All right, where does that leave us? We have two crimes— piracy and kidnapping—and no serious suspects. I think we'd better get back to the coast and dig around for more clues."

"I called my father before dinner," David said. "The police and Coast Guard haven't made any progress. I agree we should go back, but before we leave tomorrow, I'd like to take you up to Mountain Pine Ridge. It's a huge forest reserve, and it's quite lovely."

"I guess there's no great rush to get back," Nancy said. "I'd love to see it."

They went to bed soon after so they could get

up early the next morning. Nancy fell asleep regretting her fight with Ned, hoping they could make it up soon.

The air was fresh and cool the next morning as they started the drive south through the mountains, but it quickly grew hot as the sun rose higher.

They drove slowly over the rough dirt roads, until they entered the Mountain Pine Ridge reserve, leaving civilization far behind. David drove through miles of wilderness, deserted except for a few hikers and horseback riders on the nature trails. Nancy marveled at the variety of birds and butterflies she could see from the Jeep. She gazed at the expanse of pine trees covering the rolling granite mountains as Ramón talked about the Mayans who hunted there centuries earlier.

Finally David stopped the Jeep by a path and took out a couple of flashlights. They all walked down to a small stream that flowed from a waterfall above and into a limestone cave. A rich jungle of ferns, palms, and flowers crowded the banks of the stream.

"Oh, my," Becca said as they went into the cave. "This is simply too beautiful for words."

Nancy had to agree. The ceiling soared fifty feet above their heads and the floor was a sandy beach circling an almost perfectly round pool of clear water. The light was cool and dim, but they could make out fantastic stone formations carved by the once-large river many years before.

"Come on," David said. They followed, climbing jagged chunks of stones that lined the walls of the cave. With help from the flashlights, they made their way deeper inside, hopping over occasional gaps between the rocks.

"Ooohh," Becca squealed, stopping at a wide breach. "I—I just don't think I can jump that far."

"I'll help you," Ned said.

"Oh, Ned, I don't know. . . ." Becca hesitated.

Ned leapt to the far side and reached back for her while David shone his flashlight on the breach. "Come on, try it. I'll catch you."

"Well . . ." Becca, trembling, took a deep breath and then made a running jump.

Ned caught her in his arms and swung her around. "See? You're safe."

"Only thanks to you." Becca hugged him, then kissed his cheek.

Ned hugged her back. "You can trust me, Becca."

Nancy watched them, anger rising. Fuming, she trailed behind as they worked their way to the back of the cave. Finally, Nancy spotted a slit of daylight ahead. They crept out through the crack into the bright sunshine and started up a narrow path leading back to the mouth of the cave.

"Ned," Nancy called. "Can I talk to you for a minute?"

He stopped and let the others continue on. "What is it?" he asked as she caught up to him.

"I've had enough, Ned." Nancy brushed away a lacy giant fern that tickled her cheek. Behind Ned she saw a bromeliad with golden yellow flowers blooming high up in a tree and wild orchids dripping from a branch. Beauty was all around her, but she couldn't enjoy it.

"What's the matter, Nan?" he asked.

"Don't call me Nan! Not when you're carrying on like that with Becca. If you two are going to hug and kiss, at least don't do it in front of me."

"You mean in the cave? She was only grateful—"

"I don't care what *she* was. I care about how *you* feel, and it's pretty obvious to me."

"What am I supposed to do when a pretty girl hugs me?" Ned said. "Push her away? Besides, the way you and Manny were dancing at the party, it was clear you were feeling something, too!"

"I wouldn't have been dancing with Manny if you hadn't been so busy with Becca. You didn't even know I was there."

"Hi, you two," David said, coming back down the path. "We thought you might be lost. Why don't we head over to the Río On pools? It's pretty hot out and everyone needs to cool off."

Nancy and Ned got the message. Silently they followed him back to the Jeep.

A short while later they parked beside another trail. They got out of the Jeep and followed the trail down to a shallow river flowing over huge smooth boulders. To their right, the crystal-clear water spilled over a natural dam, forming a small waterfall, then flowed into a series of pools. Some were shallow, some quite deep.

"Oh, I can't wait!" Becca kicked off her sandals, stripped down to her bikini, and ran out onto a smooth boulder.

"Be careful!" David shouted after her. "These rocks are very slippery."

Becca called back, "Don't y'all worry about me. I'm—whoops!" She lost her footing and fell.

Ned started toward her, then glanced at Nancy and hesitated. It was Ramón and David who helped Becca up and fussed over her bruised knee.

Nancy stepped carefully onto a boulder. Centuries of rushing water had polished it almost as smooth as glass, and she found that below the water a fine coating of algae made the stones so slick it was impossible to walk. The easiest way to travel was to swim or crawl, she decided, depending on the depth of the pools.

"Everyone, come over here," David called. He perched on a rock in the middle of the river, then suddenly let go and slid down a natural waterslide into a deep swirling pool ten feet below.

Nancy was the next one down, soon followed by the others. The cool water felt wonderful. They laughed and splashed each other like children and took turns sitting under the six-foot waterfall, enjoying the rush of the clean river flowing over their heads.

Much later, Nancy decided to take a break. She sat down next to Ramón and watched the water swirling in the deep pool below them.

"Are you enjoying yourself, Ramón?" she asked.

"It's good to take a day away from research," he replied. "Even when I love my work."

"You said you were studying the blend of various races in the Caribbean," Nancy said. "How do you do it? Do you simply ask people who their parents are?"

"It often requires much more than that," Ramón replied. "Some know their families many generations back, some know very little."

Glancing around, Nancy noticed Becca making her way over the boulder behind them. Her right knee was mottled with a bluish red bruise from her fall.

"What do you do when people can't remember?" Nancy asked.

"If I had the money, as I hope to someday, I could use DNA studies and other advanced techniques. Now I rely on written material, such as birth records, and once in a while I take blood samples."

"Blood samples? Can you do that if you're not a doctor?" Nancy asked.

"Oh, yes, it's very easy. A tiny prick, a quick test with a simple kit, and I can type the blood.

Studies have shown that blood type can help identify race, since—"

"Watch out!" Becca screamed.

Nancy looked over her shoulder and saw Becca falling toward her. Nancy tried to grab the other girl, but Becca fell heavily against her. Nancy tumbled down the waterslide. Her head exploded in pain, and then everything went dark.

Chapter

Eight

HELP," BECCA SCREAMED. "Somebody help! Nancy's drowning!"

Becca lay sprawled on her stomach at the top of the waterslide, watching Nancy's unconscious body swirling around the deep pool, arms and legs limp.

Ramón scrambled over Becca and threw himself down the slide.

Ned, downriver, reacted the moment he heard Becca's cry. Stumbling over the slick rocks, he half ran, half slid to the pool and threw himself in.

Ramón, choking as he treaded water in the swift current, had grabbed Nancy but wasn't able to make headway to shore.

"Let me!" Ned shouted. Expertly, he flipped her over into the lifesaving hold. Swimming hard, he pulled her to the side of the pool, where David waited on a boulder.

"Take her arms," Ned said. With David pulling and Ramón and Ned pushing, the three men managed to free Nancy from the strong current. Ned and David carried her to the riverbank and gently put her down under a palm tree. Ned knelt over her and placed his ear against her heart.

"I don't think she's breathing!" He quickly pressed the artery in her neck. "But she has a faint pulse."

He tilted her chin back and breathed into her mouth twice. When he saw her chest rise, indicating there was no obstruction, he began the rescue breath. The others gathered around, stunned and silent.

Every five seconds Ned blew into Nancy's mouth, pausing after every twelve breaths to check her pulse. Endless moments passed. Ned continued the CPR.

Finally Nancy's chest heaved. Quickly Ned turned her on her side and she coughed up river water.

She groaned. "My—my head . . ."

"She's all right!" Ned sighed with relief.

Nancy stirred and tried to sit up.

"Just relax, Nan," Ned crooned, cradling her in his arms. "Don't try to move."

She blinked her eyes, relieved to see Ned's familiar face. "I fell—what happened?"

"You hit your head," Ned said. "You're going to have a monster bump, but you're okay."

"Oh, I am so sorry," Becca whispered. "I didn't mean to . . . I tried to stop—"

"You couldn't help it," Ramón said, remembering how he'd felt on the Mayan ruin. He put an arm around Becca's waist. "It was an accident."

Becca leaned her head against his chest. "I'm just so *terribly* sorry."

In a few minutes Nancy was able to sit up, although her head pounded with pain. She looked around at her friends and managed a small smile. "Looks like we've all been in a war."

Becca's stomach was scratched, her arms and legs covered with bruises from her fall. Ned's knees were skinned from scrambling over the rocks, and Ramón had a long red scrape on his side from his hasty plunge down the waterslide.

Only David was uninjured. "I think we'd better forget about getting back to the coast and spend another night at Casa Maya. Nancy needs to rest and—"

"I'm all right," Nancy protested, trying to get up. "Ugh." The sudden jolt of pain was intense.

"You need to see a doctor," David said firmly. "I'm taking you back to the lodge. We're not going anywhere tonight."

Nancy gave in, and during the long, hot, bumpy drive down the mountain she was glad she had. The throbbing in her head was fierce. When they reached the lodge, she lay down in her cool, dim room and closed her eyes.

She'd had two accidents in one day. Or were they really accidents? she wondered. Had Ramón intended to push her off the Mayan ruin? If so, why did he pull her to safety? No, she was sure that her scare was a combination of his overeager touch and her own startled reaction.

But what about Becca? Did she fall on purpose? Why would she? Maybe she wanted Nancy out of the way so she could have Ned to herself. Nancy rejected the idea immediately; Becca was not in love with Ned. Besides, Ramón had told her that Becca had yelled for help immediately.

No, Nancy decided, there was no reason to suspect that either incident was anything more than an accident. Except for eliminating Ramón as a suspect, she wasn't much closer to solving the mystery.

Discouraged by her lack of clues, she admitted to herself that the kidnappers could be anywhere. But she was still convinced that the pirates and the kidnappers were the same, and that the police search would keep them hidden somewhere in Belize.

If only she had some concrete evidence, she thought. Unless . . .

She sat up suddenly, and her head exploded with pain. Groaning, she lay back down. There was another clue, she realized. Someone had said something recently that had given her an idea. What was it?

She lay still, trying to recall the remark, but she

couldn't remember anything about it. It was maddening, knowing that she'd made a vital connection in the case, only to have it slip away from her.

The more she tried to grasp the memory, the further away it slid. She was feeling quite frustrated when the doctor arrived. After examining her, he found only a slight concussion. He gave her something for the pain, and by dinnertime Nancy felt better enough to join the others on the patio.

"My goodness, you men were amazing," Becca said as she helped herself to salad from the buffet the cook had set out. "Nancy, when you fell, Ramón went down that slide quick as a snake. And Ned, why, he just about flew over those slippery old rocks."

"Not quite flew!" Ned laughed as he pointed to his skinned knees.

"Your poor knees," Becca said in her soft drawl. "I declare, you're a real hero."

Ned blushed with pleasure and gave her a warm smile. "Not really," he said modestly.

Oh, no, Nancy thought as she carried her plate of food to the table, here we go again. After Ned's tender concern that afternoon, she had been sure they had forgotten their fight, but now she realized that he was still under Becca's spell.

"And, Nancy," Becca went on, "I just can't tell you how sorry I am. I don't know how it happened."

"It's all right, Becca," Nancy said. "You tried to warn me. I didn't react fast enough."

"Well, David," Becca said as he joined them at the table, his plate heaped high. "Yesterday you dragged me up to the top of that old ruin and gave me vertigo, and today Nancy almost drowned in your silly river." Her beautiful almond-shaped eyes sparkled with humor. "What are you planning for us tomorrow?"

David chuckled. "Nothing! I think we should all stay in bed, to be on the safe side."

Nancy joined in the laughter, then said, "In spite of the accident, I'm glad we went to Mountain Pine Ridge. I loved seeing the countryside, and I'm impressed that Belize has set aside such a huge reserve."

After dinner, Ramón excused himself to work on his papers and Becca left to "freshen up a bit." Nancy was sure Becca wore quite a bit of make-up, but she applied it so expertly that it wasn't obvious.

"How are you feeling, Nancy?" David asked her. "Is your head still hurting?"

"It's much better, thanks." She cautiously touched the swelling on her forehead. "But the fall seems to have knocked an important clue out of my mind. While I was resting before dinner I was thinking about the piracy and Cutler's kidnapping. Someone said something, either today or yesterday, that began to give me an idea, but now I can't remember what it was.

"This entire case is rather frustrating," Nancy concluded with a sigh. "How can we have two major crimes and almost no clues?"

"Well, we do have the homing transmitters found on the rafts," Ned said.

"Can you think of a single reason the pirates would want to keep track of the rafts?" Nancy asked. "Once the pirates have the yachts, why do they care about the rafts?"

Ned and David shook their heads.

"I have the feeling," Nancy said, "that our most important clue is the ear-piercing. There has to be a reason behind it."

"Excuse me," the housekeeper said. "There is a telephone call for Miss Jackson from a Mr. Lee Po."

"Thanks, Carmelita, I'll tell her to take it in the study." David went to find Becca.

Nancy and Ned were left alone. Nancy gazed at his handsome face and remembered his look of concern as he had bent over her that afternoon. "Thanks, Ned. You saved my life."

"Anytime, Nan. No problem." He flashed her his old grin, and for a moment she wondered if they could forget about their fight.

David returned and had barely sat down when Becca burst into the room.

"I have to go back." Becca's face was ashen, her eyes full of panic. "I have to get back to the coast right away!"

"What's the matter?" David asked, standing up.

"Th-there's a problem." Becca grabbed his hand. "If you can't take me, is there a bus? A plane?"

"Take it easy," David said, patting her shoulder. "I'll drive you back. What's the problem?"

"I—I—uh—" Becca glanced around the room, her eyes dark against her suddenly pale skin. "It's Chang, my cabin boy. He—he's . . . sick. Very sick. He needs me."

"Okay," David said. "We'll leave right away. Nancy, are you up to the drive? You could stay here, and I'll send a car for you tomorrow."

"No, I'm fine now," she said, and headed for the door. "I'll go get my bag."

Nancy frowned as she went down the hall to her room. Becca was clearly upset by Lee Po's call, but Nancy didn't believe her story about Chang. If the young Chinese boy actually was sick, Becca would have said so right away. Instead, it was clear to Nancy that Becca was fishing around for a reason and made up Chang's illness as an excuse to return to Belize City.

What had Lee Po said to Becca on the phone? Nancy wondered. And why was Becca lying about it?

Chapter

Nine

Rᴀᴍóɴ, ʏᴏᴜ'ʀᴇ ᴡᴇʟᴄᴏᴍᴇ to stay here at Casa Maya as long as you like," David said as they tossed their bags into the Jeep a short while later.

Ramón broke into a big smile. "That is most kind, most gracious. I don't know what to say."

"Just say 'thanks,'" David joked. "We may be back in a few days. There's still a lot in this area I want to show Nancy and Ned. In the meantime, I hope your research goes well."

Ramón waved goodbye as they drove off. Nancy sat in back with Becca, who curled up in the corner and soon fell asleep. No one spoke much. They were tired after their eventful day and content to listen to the tapes David played softly on the Jeep's stereo.

Nancy recalled the scene on the patio when Becca appeared in such a panic. Did I jump to a conclusion? she asked herself. No, she decided, she hadn't been mistaken. Becca was clearly fishing for an excuse when David asked her what the problem was.

They had almost reached the coast when Becca stirred in her sleep and muttered something. Nancy leaned closer to listen.

"No, Lee Po, how could you," Becca mumbled. ". . . don't believe it . . . please, no." She shifted position slightly and fell silent.

Nancy's heart raced. Becca sounded as though Lee Po were doing something terrible to her. On the boat Nancy had felt there was something odd about their relationship, and this seemed to confirm it.

When they reached the harbor and parked near Becca's boat, Nancy almost felt she should stop the other girl from going aboard. Was Becca really safe with Lee Po? But how could she prevent her from returning to her own boat? Nancy knew nightmares could take any shape and were hardly evidence that something was really wrong.

"Thanks, David." Becca sleepily got out and stood on tiptoe to kiss his cheek. "I sure am sorry to make y'all drive back so late in the evening."

David shrugged. "It's cooler driving at night. I hope Chang is all right. And what about you?"

"Don't worry about me. I'm a big girl who can take care of herself. See y'all later." Becca turned and hurried up the gangplank to the brightly lit deck.

When David, Ned, and Nancy arrived at Casa Playa, they went into the living room and Marie brought them steaming cups of herbal tea and banana bread fresh from the oven.

"The light is still on in my father's study," David said. "I'll go see if he has any news. Be back in a minute."

For the second time that night, Nancy and Ned found themselves alone. Nancy studied Ned for a moment and decided to tell him her suspicions.

"Ned, I'm worried about Becca." She explained why she believed Lee Po's message had nothing to do with Chang. She was about to describe the dream when Ned interrupted.

"Are you telling me you think Becca lied?" Ned jumped up and strode across the room. "She wouldn't do that. You're making this up because you don't like her."

"I'm not imagining it," Nancy said. "And I like Becca very much."

"You're jealous of her, aren't you?" Ned turned to face Nancy.

"No, I'm not," Nancy said. "She doesn't like you specially, Ned, even if you think she does. Don't you see? She flirts with all the men in exactly the same way. You're not the only one."

"I didn't say I was." Ned scowled.

"Becca is not upsetting me," Nancy said, "you are. You ignore me whenever she's around. We've been dating for a long time, Ned, and it hurts me when you act as if I don't exist."

"I haven't ignored you!" Ned said.

Nancy's temper flared. "This afternoon is the first time you've paid any attention to me when Becca's around. What do I have to do, throw myself in a river if I want you to notice me?"

"Nancy!" Ned stood still, shocked.

She watched different emotions flicker across his face, wondering what he was thinking. Perhaps he was remembering how he had felt when he had carried her limp body from the water. Was he comparing his love for her with the way he felt about Becca?

Ned's shoulders slumped. "Oh, Nan, I've been a jerk, haven't I?"

She ran to him, and he pulled her close, wrapping her tightly in his arms. They clung together, as if trying to make up for the time they'd been apart.

Ned whispered in her ear, "Can you forgive me?"

"Oh, Ned," Nancy whispered back. "Of course I forgive you. I love you."

"That's more like it!" David said from the doorway. "I thought you two would never come to your senses."

Ned glanced at Nancy ruefully. "Yeah, well, some of us are just a little slow." He led her back to the couch.

"Any news?" Nancy asked as she sat down.

David shook his head. "Still no ransom note, and the kidnappers have vanished without a trace. The police think they must have left the country. The Coast Guard is broadcasting warnings every hour and checking boats in the area, in case they're out at sea."

"Poor Mr. Cutler," Ned said. "First his yacht is hijacked, and then he's carried off somewhere in the middle of the night."

"It can't be a coincidence," Nancy said. "With Cutler the victim of both crimes, there must be a connection. When I hear from my father about his background, maybe it will give us a clue."

"Gosh, I almost forgot." David pulled a few sheets of paper out of his pocket. "Here's a fax addressed to you, Nancy."

"Thanks." She read through the pages quickly. Her father confirmed that Ramón had not graduated from any college in the United States, but she kept that to herself. Carson Drew could find no other information on him since he didn't have access to files from Castro's Cuba.

Nancy moved on to the section about Cutler. "Dad didn't find out much that's new," she told Ned and David. "But he confirms what Joe Mason said. Cutler's quite wealthy. He's also single, although he was married briefly about twenty years ago. No children. He makes the society pages frequently, always escorting a different woman, but sailing is his passion. He bought the *Windchime* five years ago and often takes long cruises."

"That's all?" Ned asked. "No hidden crimes, no scandal, no skeletons of any type in the closet?"

"No," Nancy said. "Dad says he's sorry, but

Cutler seems to be pretty average, except for his wealth."

"It looks like the motive is still money, then," Ned said. "But why haven't they asked for ransom?"

"We may hear from them soon," Nancy said. "Meanwhile, I'm still worried about Becca." She told David about her concern about Lee Po's phone call, and then she recounted what Becca had mumbled in her sleep.

"It's only a feeling, but I don't trust Lee Po. He was quite rude to Becca when we were on her boat for lunch, and whatever he said on the phone really upset her. Then that dream . . . There's something going on, and I don't like it."

"Why don't we drop by to see her in the morning?" David suggested. "Just to make sure she's all right."

"Good idea," Nancy said. "What about the rest of tomorrow? Any plans?"

"Nothing definite. I thought we might fly out to Ambergris Cay and snorkel at Hol Chan with Manny. The forecast says the wind and water are supposed to be calm."

"That's perfect," Nancy said. She didn't remind David that she was anxious to question Manny about his midnight trips and the threatening note. "I can't wait to see the reef."

"We'll leave right after we visit Becca." David yawned, then glanced at his watch. "It's late. I think I'll go up to bed and give you two a chance to finish what I interrupted a few minutes ago."

He gave them a cheery wave as he went out the door.

"You'd better go to bed, too, Nan," Ned said. "You've had a rough day." He gently caressed her cheek.

Nancy snuggled up to him. "I will in a minute, but first, what good is having a terrible fight if you can't kiss and make up afterward?"

"Nan, you are something else." He smiled into her eyes, then kissed her deeply.

It was quite a few minutes later before they finally went up to their bedrooms.

The next morning, right after breakfast, they drove down to the harbor in David's sports car. As soon as Nancy spotted *La Moola* tied up at the dock, she knew something was wrong. The curtains were drawn and a tarp covered the cockpit.

As soon as David stopped the car, Nancy ran up the gangplank and discovered she was right. No one was on board.

She went over to a small cabin cruiser tied up behind *La Moola* where a woman was mopping the deck.

"Hi," Nancy called. "We're looking for Becca Jackson. Would you happen to know where she went?"

The woman paused and leaned on her mop. "They left late last night in a powerboat. It made such a racket it woke me up."

"You said 'they.' Who was with her?" Nancy asked.

"The Chinese guy, Lee Po, and the little kid." Becca would hardly take Chang out in a boat late at night if he were really sick, Nancy thought. "Did you see which course they took?"

"Out to sea." The woman pointed at the vast shallow water dotted with small islands and the deep blue Caribbean beyond the reef.

"Thanks." Nancy returned to the car and told Ned and David what the woman had said. "Becca and little Chang could be anywhere by now," she said anxiously. "I'm worried about them. Why did she go off with Lee Po?"

"I'm sure they're all right," David said.

"I'm not," Nancy countered, folding her arms. "I don't trust that man, and my instincts tell me something is terribly wrong. I think Becca and Chang are in real danger!"

Chapter

Ten

"YOU COULD BE RIGHT, NANCY," David said. "But I have the feeling Becca can take care of herself as well as the boy. There's more to her than meets the eye."

"That's true," Nancy said. She thought about their luncheon on Becca's boat when the captain refused to let her steer. "Lee Po practically snarled at her, but she stood up to him and made him back down."

"She's too much," Ned said. "So tiny and soft-spoken, but feisty if she has to be. Kind of like a kitten." He glanced at Nancy and blushed.

"You're right, Ned," Nancy said, her smile showing she'd forgiven him. "But more like one of Manny's *jaguar* kittens. Somehow I don't see Becca as a house pet. She's too independent."

"Speaking of Manny," David said, "he's waiting for us on Ambergris Cay. You know, that might be where Becca went. Only a very few cays are inhabited, and Ambergris has the largest town. It's a logical place for her to go."

"Then we should definitely check it out," Nancy said. "Let's go."

It was a short drive to the small airport, and they were soon in the air, flying over the shallow turquoise waters. Islands were scattered around, rising barely above sea level. From north to south, as far as they could see, ran the endless line of white foam where ocean waves crashed against the barrier reef.

About ten minutes later David said, "There it is, Ambergris Cay, featuring San Pedro, the most important town on the islands."

Nancy looked to where he pointed. "That's it?" she said, teasing David. "You call that a town?" She saw a cluster of buildings grouped around a few short docks and a minuscule landing strip. The rest of the island consisted of one long road that ran down the reef side and nothing else but sand, trees, and mangrove swamps.

"Well, we do have some resorts along the coast, too," he said, faking injured pride.

Nancy kept up the game. "You call those resorts?" Scattered along the water were small hotels, none taller than two stories, plus an occasional thatch-roofed cabana on the beach. No towering high rises, no elaborate pools, golf courses, or any of the other amenities most resorts considered necessary.

Nancy smiled. "I think I'm going to like this place."

"Just wait till you see Hol Chan," David said as he prepared to touch down at the miniature airport.

Manny was waiting for them as they stepped out of the plane. "Nancy!" he cried, sweeping her up in a big bear hug.

Over Manny's shoulder Nancy saw Ned frown but when he caught her wink, he relaxed.

David arranged for the plane to be refueled, and then they walked over to the harbor, which was less than three minutes away. Nancy kept an eye open for Becca and Chang but didn't see them.

"Welcome aboard the *Manta Ray!*" Manny tossed their beach bag containing flippers, snorkels, masks, and towels onto the deck and helped Nancy into his boat.

"What a beauty," she said, looking around. The brasswork gleamed, the teak woodwork showed the sheen of frequent oiling, and the twin outboard engines had no trace of oil or salt spray to mar their shine.

"It impresses the tourists," Manny said, but Nancy could tell he was tremendously proud of his hard work.

As Manny cast off and headed out of the harbor, Nancy studied him. How could this handsome, charming Mayan, a man who risked his life to rescue jaguar kittens, be involved in anything illegal? And how could she approach him about his midnight trips and the note without hurting his feelings? She'd never felt so reluctant to question a suspect.

She'd worry about that later, Nancy decided. For the moment she decided to enjoy the snorkeling, one of her favorite sports.

They left the island behind and fifteen minutes later dropped anchor in about ten feet of water, a couple of hundred yards inside the reef. One other boat was moored farther south with a few snorkelers around it. The ocean beyond the reef was choppy with lots of whitecaps dotting the blue waves.

They quickly slipped on their fins and adjusted their masks. "Last one in is a rotten papaya!" David challenged. One after another, they jumped off the boat into the clear, warm water.

Manny insisted on swimming beside Nancy. "The tide is going out and the current can be strong, especially near the channel through the reef. You might need my help if you get tired."

Ned, knowing what a strong swimmer Nancy was, chuckled but didn't comment. Instead, he offered to pair up with David. Swimming slowly, they headed for the reef.

Nancy found herself in a different world. As she floated with her face in the water, ordinary sounds were shut out; she could hear only herself breathing through the snorkel tube. But it was the coral and the fish that transported her to a different dimension.

Just below her swam two groupers, each almost

four feet long. Striped gray and black with blunt snouts, they weren't beautiful, but their size was awesome. Kicking slowly, Nancy moved toward a wall of coral looming ahead in the distance.

Silvery pipefish, long and slender, swam just under the water's surface. Off to her right she saw what looked like an unusually large one, perhaps three feet in length. Taking a closer look at the fish's fearsome mouth, she realized it was a barracuda. It ignored her as she swam past.

Nancy reached the coral wall and found it teeming with fish of every color and shape. Sergeant majors danced nearby, their oval bodies splashed with yellow on top, as if the sun had lent them color. Spiny wrasses with bright blue heads and sea green bodies darted around coral branches.

Holding her breath, Nancy dove down along the coral wall and saw purple damselfish with golden tails, frisky blue hamlets, and a scarlet squirrelfish with huge, solemn eyes. Returning to the surface, she blew the water out of her snorkel tube. Manny, too, had resurfaced.

"Oook." Manny's speech was muffled by the mouthpiece of his snorkel tube.

Nancy followed his pointing finger. A manta ray swam just above the sandy bottom, its wings slowly undulating with incredible grace.

"Om ith me," Manny said. "Arrot ish." They put their faces in the water again as Manny led her down the reef. A huge brilliant green parrot fish with bright red fins and tail was nibbling at a stand of slender staghorn coral. It chewed up bites of coral and spit out clouds of crushed debris. Just beyond it, a giant lacy purple sea fan waved in the current.

When Nancy was sure the water was deep enough so that her flippers wouldn't brush against coral and injure it, she turned upright, treading water, and took the tube out of her mouth. "Manny, I've never seen so many varieties of fish in one place—and they're all so much bigger than usual!"

Manny removed his tube and grinned. "These are normal size. What you see around other reefs are small because the larger ones have been hunted. Come on, I know where a queen angelfish hangs out."

On the way, they passed a school of blue fish, their colors flashing from navy to iridescent cobalt as they changed direction and caught the sun's rays.

Ned and David hovered a short distance ahead, almost motionless. As Nancy swam up, she saw what fascinated them; a green moray eel, at least six feet long, made its way across the grassy bottom and disappeared into a crevice. A moment later it popped its head out, ready to defend itself against any person or fish who dared come too close.

Nancy looked at Ned and said through her mouthpiece, "Antastic."

The two pairs of swimmers moved on, closer to the point where the channel cut through to the open ocean. The pull of the outgoing tide was strong. David was closest to a coral ledge when an extra strong wave pushed them toward it.

"Ouch!" David rubbed his arm.

Manny took one look, removed his tube, and said, "Fire coral. Come on, let's go back to the boat. I have vinegar that will cut the sting."

"Man, that hurts," David muttered.

"Can you swim?" Nancy asked.

"Sure," David said. "You and Ned stay here. Don't let me spoil your fun." He and Manny quickly headed for the *Manta Ray*.

Nancy and Ned continued along the reef, keeping a safe distance from the coral. Soon she felt herself lose touch with the outside world as she became absorbed in the undersea life. She floated almost in a daze, mesmerized by the extraordinary variety and beauty around her. There was so much to see, so much she wanted to remember.

"Ned, look," she said when she realized that the enormous, rocklike shape below her was actually an incredibly ugly grouper. Getting no answer, she looked around. Ned had drifted away and was some distance down the reef.

She looked back at the boat and saw Manny leaning over David, holding a cloth to his arm.

To reach Ned, Nancy cut across the channel opening, kicking hard to fight the drag of the current. Glancing at the dark water beyond the channel, she was surprised to see a scuba diver emerging from the ocean side. He wore a hooded black wet suit and carried a speargun.

Nancy knew hunting was strictly prohibited at Hol Chan. She wondered if the scuba diver realized where he was. Waving her arms, she tried to signal him.

The diver saw her and headed in her direction, holding the speargun in front of him. She kept signaling, pointing to the gun and shaking her head "No."

He kept coming. Suddenly Nancy realized he was pointing the speargun right at her. Then he took aim and fired!

Chapter

Eleven

Nancy dove violently to the side as the spear shot toward her. She heard a sharp slicing sound as it whizzed past, missing her chest by inches.

The scuba diver paused to reload, but Nancy didn't dare take the time to call for help. Kicking furiously, she turned and began to swim parallel to the reef. If she tried to make it back to the boat, she would be slowed down by fighting the tide.

She glanced back over her shoulder. The diver was swimming hard against the outgoing tide, heading straight for her. Just ahead, ten feet under the surface, she saw a growth of brain coral the size of a small cottage. Taking in a lungful of air, she dove down and swam to the far side.

As Nancy circled behind the mammoth round coral, she caught another glimpse of the diver. It was hard to make out the features of the person behind the mask. She saw only the gleam of dark eyes before she ducked behind the coral.

She kept swimming, trying to keep the mound of coral between her and the diver.

Nancy's lungs began to ache for air. She'd have to surface soon. Because of the tanks on his back, the scuba diver had no such problem.

Where was Ned? she wondered. If she shouted, would David and Manny hear her on the boat?

Her chest thumped with pain. She had to breathe! Spotting a forest of elkhorn coral behind her, she raced for its protection. Darting behind the broad, antlerlike branches, she saw the diver's fins disappearing behind the brain coral. He must have changed direction, hoping to catch her by surprise.

Nancy burst to the surface, gulping air into her starved lungs. Her chest heaving, she finally found breath enough to shout.

"Ned, David—help!" Dipping her face under the surface, she saw the diver aiming the speargun at her again.

She filled her lungs and dove for the bottom. The spear hissed past her, nicking her left flipper. To her right was shallow water, surrounded by coral. She could be trapped unless she found a passage out. To her left was deeper water, but it offered no protection unless she stayed close to the sand and zigzagged between the scattered chunks of coral that dotted the seabed.

She didn't have a second's worth of breath to

waste. Veering left, she dove deep, heading toward the nearest coral clump. Looking over her shoulder, she saw the diver coming after her. Her heart pounding, her legs kicking fiercely, she dashed for cover. She darted behind a cluster of coral just as another spear zipped through the water overhead.

As she crouched with aching lungs, she suddenly realized that the last spear had come from the opposite direction. Looking up, she saw two swimmers above her. Manny and David. And Manny had a speargun.

She looked back. The scuba diver was retreating. Nancy sprang off the seabed and raced for the surface. She burst through the water into the sunlight, and sucked in greedy gulps of air. Gasping and panting, she treaded water, watching Manny and David track the scuba diver toward the channel leading out to the ocean. Ned was far down the reef, still innocently enjoying himself, completely unaware of the attack.

Manny and David turned back just short of the spot where waves broke over the reef. When they got nearer to Nancy, Manny removed his tube and shouted, "Are you all right?"

"Yes, thanks to you." Her breathing had almost returned to normal. "Where is he?"

"He slipped back through the channel. It's too dangerous to try to follow him without scuba gear," David said.

"I think I see a small white powerboat anchored out in the ocean," Nancy said. "But the water's so choppy and full of whitecaps, it's hard to be sure."

"I have binoculars on the boat," Manny said. "Let's go!"

They swam quickly back to the *Manta Ray* and climbed aboard. Manny grabbed the binoculars from a locker, and Nancy pointed, saying, "Can you see that small white boat bobbing among the whitecaps?"

Manny focused the binoculars. "Yes, he's climbing on board . . . he's starting the engine . . . he's taking off, headed north." After a moment or two he said, "Now I've lost him."

"Could you see his face?" Nancy asked.

"No, he kept the mask on," Manny replied. "But I think I recognize the boat. It comes into San Pedro for supplies, and I've also seen it out by the reef late at night. An Asian guy is always at the wheel."

"Could it be Lee Po?" Nancy wondered out loud. She thought back to the glimpse she'd had of the eyes behind the diver's mask. Yes, they definitely could have been Asian.

"Quitting so soon, Nancy?" Ned called in a teasing voice. He hung on to the boarding ladder, lazily flapping his flippers. "That's not like you. You usually snorkel for hours."

She made a face. "It wasn't my idea."

"You might say a speargun changed her mind," David said. "You missed all the fun, Ned."

"What happened?" Ned asked, concerned.

"Come aboard and we'll tell you," Manny offered.

Ned was pale under his suntan by the time they'd filled him in on the attack. "I didn't hear you call, Nancy. I must have been diving down to get a closer look at a fish just then. I feel like such an idiot!"

"It was partly my fault," she said. "We both know we should stick together in the buddy system. We shouldn't have let ourselves become separated."

David looked at her with open admiration. "I can't believe you managed to avoid that speargun for so long. You must be some swimmer."

"She is." Ned hugged her tightly. "She sure is," he repeated, kissing her cheek.

Nancy hugged him back, then looked at Manny. "I was glad to see you have a speargun, too. Do you do a lot of hunting?"

"Um, not really." Manny avoided her gaze. "Once in a while, when I take a scuba party out—but not at Hol Chan, of course."

"Do you ever take groups out night fishing?" Nancy asked.

He gave her a swift glance then looked away. "Sometimes."

"Hey, Manny," David said. "What gives? I know you, old chum. You look just the way you did in school when the teacher caught you shooting spitballs. What have you been up to?"

Manny studied his best friend, then sighed. "You won't like it."

"Try me," David urged. "I never told on you in school."

"That's because you shot many spitballs yourself." Manny's grin flashed, then faded. "Okay, but you're going to be angry." He sighed again. "Some nights I go out for parrot fish."

"But they're protected now," David said. "You're breaking the law."

"It's a stupid law." Dark fire flashed in Manny's eyes. "Tourists love them, but in some spots they're eating up the reef. My ancestors were here thousands of years before you foreigners ever heard of America, and we know that the natural harmony must be preserved."

"Manny, you can't break the law," David countered. "You'll get in trouble. You know—"

"Yes, I *know*," Manny interrupted. *"But I know I'm right.* I'm out here every day. I see what too many parrot fish do to the reef."

Nancy was grateful that David had uncovered the truth behind Manny's midnight trips, but she hated to see the two close friends fighting. She put her hand on Manny's shoulder to calm him. "What do you do with the fish after you catch them?"

"I could sell them for a good price, but I don't," Manny responded in a quieter voice. "The gourmet markets pay well, but that would be wrong. I do it to protect the reef, not to make money. Instead, I eat them, and sometimes I share them with my friends."

"Maybe you shouldn't be fighting on your own," Nancy suggested. "Why not work with the government and try to get the law changed?"

"I'm doing that, too." His jaw set in a stubborn line. "I'm drafting a letter now, hoping to convince key people that something must be done."

Nancy suddenly smiled in relief. She reached into her purse and pulled out the note Manny had left in his shirt pocket. "Is this part of the letter you're writing?"

Manny frowned. "Where did you find that?"

"In your shirt pocket." She read aloud, " 'The danger is serious . . .' You meant the danger to the reef?"

"Of course." Manny took the paper. " 'This is not a joke . . .' Can you believe some people laugh at me when I show my concern? 'Can't wait any longer . . . act now or I will have to . . .' I'm having a hard time finding the right words to express myself."

David shook his head. "Manny, Manny, what am I going to do with you? Why didn't you ask me to help? I know these people, and I know how to make them see the light. You're such a stubborn, proud fool."

"You sound like my mother." Manny chuckled. "Okay, I'll let you help. Come for dinner and we'll work on the letter. And I'll serve you the best fish you've ever tasted. Parrot fish!"

A grin spread across David's face. "You're an old rogue."

"And proud of it," Manny gave David an affectionate slap on the back. "Now, Nancy, you were starting to say something about that guy who attacked you. What did you call him?"

"Lee Po," she said. "Of course, I can't be sure it was he." She explained to Manny why the man made her uneasy. "But if it was, how did he know I was here?"

"Maybe he saw you in San Pedro boarding my boat," Manny suggested. "Or someone could have told him. It's a very small town, and now that the tourist season is over, there aren't too many outsiders around. Plus, a beautiful young woman does tend to attract attention."

"Thanks." She smiled, then looked thoughtful. "If Becca mentioned to Lee Po that I'm a detective, and if he's up to no good, he might think I came to spy on him. That could be a reason for the attack."

"If it is Lee Po, Becca must be with him," Ned said. "They could be somewhere near here, or at least within a powerboat's cruising range."

"I noticed several extra gas tanks on that boat," Manny said. "It's equipped to go a long distance, and it's fast. They could be anywhere. There are hundreds—thousands—of small and large cays strung out along the coast."

"Cays where pirates or kidnappers could easily hide," Nancy commented.

"And where they could remain hidden for a very long time if they had enough supplies," Manny declared.

With this glum assessment of the situation they fell silent, sitting on the *Manta Ray* as it gently rocked at anchor.

David broke the spell. "I'm hungry. Let's go ashore for lunch. And I'm going to call the police and report the attack on Nancy."

"You got it," Manny said, as he started the motor.

They stopped at one of the small hotels on the shore south of town. David went with Nancy to phone the police in Belize City. Unfortunately, it was Sergeant Cordova who took her call.

"File a report in San Pedro," he said with the same note of disdain Nancy had noticed when she showed him Robert Cutler's missing pillow. "No need to hurry," he went on. "Your attacker has vanished, so enjoy your lunch first."

"I'm not sure he believes me," Nancy told David after she hung up. "He thinks I'm only a silly tourist."

"I'm going to call my father," David stated angrily. "He'll believe you, and he'll see that the police treat this matter seriously." David dialed his father's number but was told that Mr. Peck wasn't due back in his office for a couple of hours. David left a message and promised Nancy they'd call again from San Pedro.

They rejoined Ned and Manny, and the foursome ate lunch under a thatched roof on a patio by an oval swimming pool where several children splashed in the shallow end. While they enjoyed spicy chicken with rice and beans, they watched the children chase a three-foot iguana that had waddled out from under a bush. The iguana took off, its speed amazingly fast, and climbed a sloping coconut palm until it was out of their reach.

Nancy kept thinking about Lee Po and Becca. "David, could we search the cays from your airplane? We might be able to spot that power-boat tied up somewhere."

"We could try," he said. "But it's easy to hide a boat that small, especially if it's on Cay Caulker or one of the other settled islands. It would be just one of many powerboats, or they could simply throw a tarp over it and we'd never see it."

"But if Lee Po comes into San Pedro to get supplies, it probably means they're *not* in an inhabited area," Nancy said.

"As a matter of fact, one of his main purchases is jugs of water," Manny said thoughtfully. "I'll bet you're right, Nancy, but there are so many isolated cays it could take us forever to find him."

"I'm worried about Becca," Nancy said. "Do you think Lee Po lured her into a trap?"

"If he did," Ned said, "he may be the one who kidnapped Cutler, too."

"But why?" Nancy asked. "And how are these disappearances related to the piracy? I'm sure there's a connection, but I can't pin it down."

A little girl climbed out of the pool and began to chase her baby brother. The toddler tripped and burst into tears. When his mother scooped him up, Nancy saw blood trickling from a cut on his knee.

"Blood!" Nancy said suddenly. "Now I remember. Ramón was telling me about taking blood samples to trace family lines. That was just before Becca slipped and I was knocked down the waterslide. It's come back to me now. I was wondering if the pirates used the ear-piercing as a cover for typing blood."

"What do you mean?" Ned asked.

Nancy leaned forward. "The last time I donated blood, I was surprised that they pricked my ear instead of my finger when they needed a drop to check the type. Ramón said it was quick and easy to run the test with a simple kit, and it occurred to me that might be what the hijackers were after. They could take a blood sample without anyone guessing what they were really up to."

"But why would the pirates be interested in blood types?" David frowned.

"I don't know." Nancy leaned back in her chair. "Maybe one of them is injured or sick and has a rare type. Maybe they're afraid to take him to a hospital and risk arrest, so they're looking for a donor."

"I've seen your ideas pay off before, Nan," Ned said. "But you have to admit, this one is a little far out."

"It's just a possibility," she said with a wry smile. Then she stood up. "Let's get back to San Pedro so I can file a report about the attack. Maybe the police there will be more interested than Sergeant Cordova is."

As Manny guided the boat up the coast, Nancy gazed out over the water that separated the cay from the mainland. She remembered how incredible the snorkeling was and promised herself she'd go again soon—and she hoped it would be without a hooded scuba diver trying to shoot her with a speargun.

They were just pulling up to the pier in San Pedro when she caught a glimpse of a white powerboat behind some fishing boats tied farther down the shore. While the men secured the *Manta Ray,* Nancy leapt onto the dock and raced up the beach.

The powerboat was pulling away from the pier with a thin, short, dark-haired man at the wheel. Nancy saw something dark and rubbery—like a wet suit—stuffed under bags of groceries and plastic water jugs in the bow. The man glanced back at shore, and Nancy got a good look at him.

It was Lee Po!

Chapter
Twelve

Lᴇᴇ Pᴏ sᴘᴏᴛᴛᴇᴅ Nᴀɴᴄʏ at that same instant. He looked startled, and then he quickly gunned the engine. The powerboat leapt forward and tore off, heading south.

Nancy ran back to Manny's boat. "I saw him! It's definitely Lee Po. We have to follow him."

Manny frowned. "His boat's much faster than mine. We couldn't keep up."

"David, your plane!" Nancy said. "We'll track him from the air. Come on, let's go."

"Are you sure it's Lee Po, Nancy?" Ned asked. "Why would he come back to San Pedro if he's the one who attacked you?"

"His boat is loaded with water and groceries," Nancy replied. "He must have come to town to stock up but saw me, or heard I was here, and decided to go after me first. I guess he realized afterward that he still needed supplies. He *must* be involved in the piracies and kidnappings," she continued eagerly. "Why else would he have tried to hurt me? He wants me off the case. Come on, let's hurry before he gets away again."

After a hasty goodbye to Manny, Ned and David followed Nancy as she jogged the short distance to the airstrip nearby. David's plane was gassed up, ready to go, and in minutes they were in the air. Nancy sat in the copilot's seat, with Ned right behind her. "I see him," she said, pointing at a white speck down on the water. "He's going so fast he's leaving quite a wake behind."

David nodded. "I see him, too."

"We can't let him realize that we're following, or he won't lead us to where he's keeping Becca —and maybe even Cutler," she said. "With that long white wake against the blue water, we should be able to track him from a fairly high altitude."

David nodded as he put the plane into a steep climb.

"Also," Nancy said, "we should take a different course instead of following directly behind him. If you head west for a couple of minutes, David, he'll assume we're not on his trail. Then we can turn back, and he'll probably think it's a different plane, going in a different direction."

"Won't he recognize our markings?" Ned asked.

"Only if he bothers to look," Nancy said, "and

he probably can't see them from this distance. But anyway, I doubt he'd suspect we're in a plane. He'd expect us to follow him by boat, *if* we're going to follow him at all. When he doesn't see a boat in pursuit, he'll probably think he's safe."

David flew west toward the mainland until they lost sight of the powerboat's wake. Nancy was betting that Lee Po wouldn't duck into a lagoon. Since he had extra fuel tanks on board, she guessed he probably had a distance to go.

"I'd turn back now, David," Nancy suggested. "We must be out of his sight. Is there a logical course for you to take? A cay where a plane might be heading?"

"Cay Chapel," David said. "It's got a long airstrip, and Lee Po could just think we're heading in for a landing."

"Great," Nancy said. "That's perfect."

They soon spotted the powerboat's wake and flew past it. They made the same zigzag maneuver several times until they finally saw the wake lead up to a small, heavily overgrown cay.

"I don't see the boat," Ned reported. "But the wake leads right to shore."

"I see a faint line of water reflecting under the overgrowth. It connects with that large lagoon in the center of the island," Nancy said. "It looks like a channel has been cut through the trees."

"I'm putting down the flotation gear," David announced. "Where do you think I should land?"

"A good distance from the island," Nancy replied. "Then we can taxi in closer. Lee Po will hear our engine, but he'll probably assume it's a boat. He won't be suspicious since no one has followed him from San Pedro."

"This island looks different from most of the other cays," Ned observed as David began the descent.

"I was thinking the same thing," Nancy said. "There are a lot more trees, instead of sand and bushes. They're so thick I can't see any buildings, not even a hut."

"Maybe Lee Po is making only a brief stop on his trip," David suggested as he brought the plane down to a smooth landing on the water. "What if Becca and Chang aren't here?"

"We'll soon find out," Nancy said. "May we use the plane's life raft? Ned and I can row in through the channel while you stay here. We don't want to leave the plane unattended."

"Why don't you stay, Nancy?" David offered. "It would be a lot safer. Ned and I will go."

"Thanks," she said. "But I want to see what Lee Po is up to. Don't worry, we'll be careful. We'll just take a quick look and come right back."

David tried to argue, but Nancy was firm. A short while later, he stopped the engines when they were still a good distance from the island, and Nancy and Ned rowed the life raft to the channel opening.

As they crept into the tunnel-like passage, a scarlet-and-gold parrot screeched and flew down the channel ahead of them. Nancy admired the flash of its bright colors against the dark foliage. "Look, Ned," she whispered as they rowed along slowly. "The branches on top are beginning to wilt. They're dead clippings. They've been cut and hung from the living trees on the sides."

Ned studied the ten-foot-wide channel. "Someone has gone to a lot of trouble. You can see how the cuttings are tied together to form a canopy. I guess they'd have to be replaced often, too, whenever they turn brown."

"And the channel is much wider than necessary for Lee Po's little powerboat." Nancy kept her whisper so soft that Ned could barely hear her. "You could bring a good-size yacht through here. I'm beginning to guess what we're going to find, aren't you?"

Ned nodded. They silently made their way along. The only sound was the drip of water from the oars as they glided closer to the center of the island.

A couple of minutes later the channel opened to a large, deep lagoon. They stopped inside the covering vegetation and gasped at the sight before their eyes.

"Wow," Nancy whispered.

A gleaming cabin cruiser was tied to a dock on one shore of the lagoon. It looked ready to sail at any moment. Opposite it, a crew of eight or nine men swarmed over a large sailboat. One group was adding a new pole to hold the rigging to the front; another was cutting the cabin roof down to a lower silhouette. Two men were repainting the white hull a dark blue.

Nancy realized that the changes being made would alter the yacht enough to make it almost impossible to identify from a distance.

"Do you see?" Ned asked, barely breathing the words.

Nancy nodded. The painters had not yet reached the sailboat's stern where the name *Windchime* was emblazoned in gold lettering. It was Robert Cutler's yacht.

Above the boats, protecting them from being seen by anyone flying over the island, were more cut tree branches. In some places, entire palm trees were propped up, their dead fronds turning orange, yellow, and brown. Interwoven among them were fresh green leaves.

Hidden back from the lagoon, surrounded by foliage, were a number of small, thatch-roofed huts. More thatch covered a larger open cooking-and-dining area.

Nancy nudged Ned and pointed. The young boy, Chang, was unloading the last of the water jugs from Lee Po's speedboat. He was whistling and seemed happy and, Nancy noticed, quite healthy.

Ned mouthed the name "Becca," and Nancy nodded, agreeing that she must be here, too.

Nancy pointed up the channel, and Ned dipped the oars in the water. It was time to get back and report what they had discovered.

But the raft wouldn't move. It seemed to be caught on something.

A second later Lee Po's head emerged from the water. He was holding the raft's mooring line. "Hello, Ms. Drew." His grin was chilling. "Welcome to our island paradise."

Chapter

Thirteen

"Lee Po!" Nancy gasped in surprise. Her first thought was to jump out of the raft and swim back up the channel. Then she saw two men standing on the pond's edge. They held rifles, aimed at Nancy and Ned.

"Come along, Ms. Drew, Mr. Nickerson." Lee Po waded out of the water, towing the raft behind him.

Nancy and Ned had no choice. They stepped out of the raft onto shore, put their hands up as ordered, and followed Lee Po to a small thatch-roofed hut set back in the trees a distance from the others. Nancy could sense the rifles aimed at her back and was careful not to make any sudden moves.

Lee Po opened the door of the hut. Just then a scarlet-and-gold parrot flew up and landed on his shoulder. Lee Po noticed Nancy's look of surprise.

"This is Mrs. Wu," he said. "She is our watchdog, or should I say watchbird? It was she who announced you had come to visit. Isn't that right, Mrs. Wu?" He stroked the parrot's feathers.

The parrot squawked and Lee Po laughed. "She speaks only Chinese. In English it means, 'I'm a good bird.' He said something to the bird in Chinese. "Yes, Mrs. Wu, you are a most good bird."

Nancy had to smile, in spite of the situation. "I've been captured before, but never by a parrot. How did you train her to stand guard?"

"I raised her from a little chick." Lee Po gently rubbed her head. "I notice she always flies if strangers come near, so I taught her—very slowly, with much patience—to stay where I put her, and then fly to me to give warning."

"You're a clever man, Mr. Lee," Nancy said.

He grinned, beaming at her praise. "Okay, Mrs. Wu." He pointed toward the channel and said something in Chinese, apparently an order. The parrot flew off and disappeared under the canopy of greenery.

"After you, my friends." Lee Po ushered Ned and Nancy into the hut.

Nancy blinked as she stepped into the dim light, trying to adjust her eyes after the bright glare outside. A man lay on a cot, gagged and bound by the hands and feet. He raised his head from the pillow, and she realized who it was.

"Mr. Cutler, are you all right?" Nancy asked with concern.

He nodded but flashed angry eyes at Lee Po. The hut was sparsely furnished. Aside from the cot, Nancy saw a packing crate, a plastic jug half full of water, a tin basin, with nothing but a comb beside it. The hut was stiflingly hot and humid, with the only ventilation coming from the open door. Both windows had been boarded over from the outside.

Lee Po barked an order, and one of the guards took two pieces of rope from his pocket. The other stood in the doorway, his rifle aimed at the prisoners.

"Please, would you put your hands behind your back," Lee Po requested politely.

"Where is Becca?" Nancy asked as the guard tied Ned's hands together. "Is she okay?"

Lee Po laughed. "She's good, most okay. How do you like my little business here? Pretty smart, hey?"

"Very shrewd," Nancy agreed, deciding to flatter him. "What do you do with the yachts once you've altered them?"

"Sell them in Asia," Lee Po boasted. "I have contacts with a broker who pays us well—and in cash. Already two boats are on their way to Hong Kong, and we have made a most happy profit from them. Once we sell these two remaining, I will retire, for a time at least."

Robert Cutler made muffled noises of outrage.

Lee Po looked at him. "Please, Mr. Cutler, you

are a wealthy man. You can buy another yacht and call it *Windchime II*. You must not be selfish."

Nancy realized exactly what the victims of the hijackings had meant when they described the pirate leader as eerily polite. Without a doubt, Lee Po was that man. He also seemed very proud of his operation, and Nancy decided to continue playing on his vanity.

"Your crew certainly is efficient," she commented as the guard, having finished with Ned, began to tie her hands behind her back. "You've trained them well."

"Thank you." Lee Po made a slight bow.

"Where do they come from?" Nancy asked.

"We were all aboard a ship going from mainland China to New York when we ran into a bad storm and were thrown off course," Lee Po said. "Of course we did not have official papers, but we were excited, heading for the land of Golden Opportunity."

Nancy understood that he meant they were illegal aliens being smuggled into the United States.

"The ship went down, but many of us survived," Lee Po continued. "We had nothing— everything went to the bottom of the sea. A few found jobs when we came ashore. Later, some managed to set up small shops. When I thought of this boat idea, I found some of my friends and trained them in the skills they need. You see, I am providing work to many who would otherwise live in poverty."

"Of course," Nancy said, hoping he didn't hear the note of sarcasm in her voice.

Nancy saw the guard slip a gag over Ned's mouth. She knew Ned wanted to fight it off, but he didn't dare. Lee Po might be polite and willing to boast about his pirate business, but there was a steely glint in his eye. He wouldn't hesitate to order the guard to fire if necessary.

Before she, too, could be gagged Nancy quickly asked a question. "You were the scuba diver who shot at me when we were snorkeling. Why did you try to kill me?"

Lee Po went stiff with anger. "You are too nosy, Ms. Drew. And too smart. You should not have come to the cays. You almost saw me in San Pedro. It was only luck I saw you first. You should be sorry I missed shooting you. Then your boyfriend would not also be in trouble." He strode to the door. "Gag her," he ordered the guard.

Nancy tasted the oily rag as it was shoved in her mouth. The guard tied the cloth behind her head and went out, shutting the door behind him. The temperature in the hut immediately began to rise to an almost unbearable level. "Eeeel own," Ned said through his gag.

Nancy understood. She knelt behind Ned and placed her mouth against his bound hands, grateful that Lee Po hadn't thought to tie their legs, too. Ned's fingers fumbled with her gag, trying to loosen it. She turned her head and he was able to slide one finger under the knot in the back. Tugging, he managed to pull the gag up and off. She spit out the foul cloth.

"Yuck! Thanks, Ned," she said. "Now let me help you."

They reversed positions, and Nancy worked the gag off him. He licked his lips and swallowed several times to moisten his dry mouth. "Boy, what a relief."

"Your turn, Mr. Cutler," Nancy said.

When Cutler's gag was freed, it took a minute before he could talk. At last he croaked, "Thanks. They only put the gag on when you arrived, but it feels like forever."

Nancy wriggled her hands. The cord was tight around her wrists. "Ned, let's stand back to back. I'll try to free you."

"Your hands are smaller," Ned said. "I can probably get you loose quicker than you can me." He stood behind her but was so much taller their hands didn't meet. "If we sit down, I can reach you." They arranged themselves back to back on the dirt floor and Nancy felt Ned's fingers working on the knots. "Mr. Cutler, have you been tied up like this ever since you were kidnapped?" Nancy asked, knowing how painful the position was.

"No, at first I was allowed to roam around, always with a guard, of course," Cutler said. "They were pretty decent to me. Then late yesterday afternoon I saw a chance to escape. I almost made it, too. I swam underwater out through the channel, but that blasted parrot saw me and raised a ruckus. Lee Po came after me in the powerboat, and it was all over."

"I knew parrots were smart," Nancy declared. "But that Mrs. Wu is something!" She thought a moment. "Have you seen a girl named Becca?"

"The only female I've seen is a young lady who came in here this morning," Cutler said with a frown. "She didn't say anything, just stood in the doorway staring at me. I asked who she was, but she didn't answer. She just stood and stared, then left. It was creepy."

"Was she tiny, with long dark hair and beautiful eyes?" Nancy asked.

"Yes, that's a good description of her," he answered.

"It must be Becca," Nancy said eagerly. "I'm surprised Lee Po let her visit you."

"There was a guard behind her," Cutler told her. "She's probably allowed to walk around the way I could until I tried to escape."

"I'm glad to hear you were treated all right," Nancy said.

"Oh, yeah, it was great fun," Cutler said bitterly. "I just loved watching them tear my beautiful *Windchime* apart. She had such graceful lines, and they've practically destroyed her."

"You'll get her back," Nancy said, reassuring him. "Then you can restore her to her original condition."

"You have a lot more confidence than I do,"

Cutler replied, sounding discouraged. "We're helpless here."

"Ned," Nancy asked, "how long has it been since we left the plane?"

"I'm not sure. Maybe twenty minutes." His fingers kept tugging at the rope around her wrists, but it didn't feel as if he'd made any progress.

"David must be getting worried." She explained to Cutler about tracking Lee Po from the air. "I hope he doesn't decide to come after us. He'll only be captured, too, thanks to Mrs. Wu."

"You told him to radio for help if anything went wrong," Ned said. "I'm sure that's what he'll do."

"Maybe," she said. Privately she wondered if David could resist the temptation to make a dashing rescue attempt on his own.

"Curse this ear," Cutler said suddenly. He rubbed the side of his head against the pillow. "I think it's infected. It itches like mad."

"Did you get bitten?" Nancy asked.

"No, those idiots punched a hole in my other ear." Cutler was so angry he was almost spitting. "At least I wouldn't let them put another stupid earring in."

"Why would they pierce the other ear?" Nancy responded, surprised.

"I asked them, and they said they were 'making sure.'" Cutler said. "'Making sure of what?' I asked. They just laughed."

"Who did it?" Nancy asked. "Was it Lee—"

She was interrupted when the door suddenly

swung open, letting in a welcome gust of fresh air.

Becca stepped into the hut. She smiled at Nancy and ruffled Ned's hair with affection as she walked past him.

"Becca!" Nancy said. "Are you all right?"

"We were so worried about you," Ned said.

She didn't answer. Instead, she walked over to the cot and stood looking down at Robert Cutler.

"Well, Daddy," she said softly, "I guess the time has finally come. I'd like to introduce myself. I'm your long-lost daughter, Rebecca Cutler!"

Chapter

Fourteen

"Y<small>OU-YOU'RE</small> *WHAT?*" Robert Cutler sputtered.

Becca smiled patiently, as if he were a little dense. "Your daughter. I'm the baby you forced my mother to give up for adoption."

"Baby? What baby? I don't know what you're talking about." Cutler's face turned red with outrage.

"Yes, you do." Becca gave him a superior smile. "Don't you dare deny me again. You got rid of me once, but now you have no choice. I'm your daughter, and you are going to admit it in the presence of witnesses." She pointed to Nancy and Ned.

"You're crazy, young lady," Cutler said. "I've never seen you before. And I've never fathered a baby."

"How dare you lie to me!" Becca, suddenly

furious, kicked the bottom of the cot. Cutler winced.

"Becca," Nancy said sharply. "Take it easy." She was as surprised as Cutler by Becca's claim, but she knew she had to calm the girl. "Please, Becca, you have to understand that we're confused. You told us your father was an oil millionaire named Jackson."

"Ha!" Becca replied bitterly. "And you believed me. Yes, I grew up with the Jacksons, and their daddy paid for me to go to the same posh schools as his kids, but I lived in a little apartment over the garage with my mother—my adoptive mother—who cooked three meals a day for the fat, rich Jackson brats!"

She kicked the cot again, almost knocking it over. Cutler yelped. "And it's all your fault," she told him. "Because you didn't want me."

"Let me get this straight," Nancy said slowly, trying to divert Becca's attention from Cutler. "Your mother was the Jacksons' cook. And you were adopted by her."

"Yes," Becca said more quietly. "She and my father—at least the man I always thought was my father—kept it a secret. When he died two years ago I was sorting through his papers, and I found the adoption certificate."

"What did you do?" Nancy asked.

A wave of sadness washed over Becca's face. "I made my mother tell me the truth. She cried a lot, then she finally explained how they had adopted me as an infant in Miami. They moved to Louisiana soon after, hoping I'd never find out."

"But you did," Nancy said with sympathy. "What did you do then?"

"I ran away," Becca explained. "Or at least that's how my mother—my adoptive mother—took it. I packed a knapsack and hitchhiked to Mexico. After a while I worked my way down here to Central America. That's when I met Lee Po in a small village. He was working in the fields, harvesting sugarcane. It's miserable work, and it pays almost nothing. I knew right away he was too clever and too ambitious to be stuck in that job forever."

"Is that when he got the idea to hijack yachts?" Nancy asked.

"No!" Becca snorted. "Did he tell you it was his idea? That little sneak always wants to take credit. The idea was *mine*. I came back here to Belize, found him, and asked if he wanted to help me. But that didn't happen until a few months ago, when I began to look for my father."

"I'm not sure I follow you," Nancy said.

"While I was here in Belize the first time, I realized I had to find my real mother, my birth mother." Becca began to pace around the small hut as she talked. "Don't get me wrong, I love my mother—the mother who raised me—but I had to know where I came from, *who* I came from."

Nancy hoped Becca wouldn't notice that Ned was still working on the rope that tied her hands. She could feel the cord beginning to loosen a tiny bit. Fortunately, Becca was so wrapped up in her story that she didn't seem to wonder why they were sitting back to back.

"And did you find your birth mother?" Nancy encouraged Becca to go on.

"Eventually, yes, in a small hospital in Miami." Becca stopped at the open door and, preoccupied, shooed the guard away with a wave of her hand. He saluted and left. Becca barely noticed.

"She was very sick." Becca's lovely eyes glittered with tears. "She was dying of cancer. She looked a lot like me. . . ."

"Was she glad to see you?" Nancy asked.

"Oh, yes." One tear spilled over and ran down Becca's cheek. "But she wouldn't tell me who my father was. She said he would reject me, just as he had rejected us both twenty years ago. He forced her to put me up for adoption, then later he divorced her. She begged me not to look for him. She said I would only be hurt."

Becca turned and stared at Cutler from across the room. "And she was right. He denies I even exist."

Cutler struggled to sit up, not an easy task with both his hands and his feet tied together. "Look, young lady, this is an interesting story, but you've got the wrong man. I'm not your father."

"Oh, yes, you are!" Becca's fury exploded again. "And I can prove it."

"How?" Cutler demanded.

"My mother gave me three clues, although she

didn't realize it. We talked and talked, day after day, while she lay in that white hospital bed."

"What were the three clues?" Nancy asked, watching the tears running freely down Becca's cheeks.

"She had kept an eye on you," she told Cutler. "It wasn't hard. Your picture was always in the society pages, going to charity dinners, dances, the theater, while she struggled to support herself as a waitress. She said she'd read you were cruising in the Caribbean for three months. Once she let that slip out, I knew where to look."

"Is that why you've gone from island to island?" Nancy asked.

Becca nodded. "I went to every port, searching for a wealthy American sailor, forty-two years old—that was the second clue she dropped—who lived in Miami. There are an awful lot of American men down here, but I could rule out most of them. Of the ones left, we followed them when they put out to sea, and then we hijacked them. They had to pass the final test."

"What was that?" Nancy asked.

Becca smiled, her tears now gone. "My mother's third hint gave me the idea. One day she became very sick and needed a blood transfusion. While the nurse was hanging the bottle, my mother said she hoped I'd inherited her blood type, in case I ever had an accident, because my father had a rare type, AB negative, and it wasn't always easy to find the right donor."

"The ear-piercing!" Nancy said. "I guessed it,

but I couldn't imagine why you would do it. You were testing the men for their blood type."

"Yes," Becca admitted. "We took samples from all the men on board, not just anyone I suspected, to help cover up the real reason."

"You overheard Ramón telling me about taking blood samples," Nancy said. "That's why you knocked me down the waterslide. Becca, you pushed me on purpose, didn't you?"

Becca shrugged. "Sorry about that. At least I called for help. I didn't want to hurt you, but I couldn't let you start thinking. You would have made the connection. You're too smart, Nancy."

Nancy felt a little slack in the ropes around her wrist. She couldn't let Becca notice what Ned was doing. She had to keep her talking about herself. "How did you type the blood?" Nancy asked.

"It was easy," Becca replied, with a dismissive wave. "You put the blood sample on a glass slide, add a drop of reagent, mix it with an orange stick, and if it's the right type, it clumps up almost instantly." She walked over to Cutler and looked down at him. "You have AB negative blood. Only three percent of the population has it. You fit all three requirements. You are my father."

"Oh, yeah?" he said sarcastically. "If you thought I was your father, why did you dump Joe and me in the life raft and let us float around the ocean for three days?"

"That stupid Lee Po!" Becca whirled around and began to pace again. "I didn't know you were the one right away. We always made up two slides from each person, in case one was dropped or ruined with salt spray. Lee Po, the idiot, got mixed up and gave me both slides from Joe Mason. I didn't notice the mistake until you and the raft were gone. Both slides came out O negative. That's not exactly a rare type but it's unusual, and it seemed odd that both of you would have it. I tested the other slides and— bingo—AB negative."

"Is that why you put homing transmitters in the rafts, in case you needed to track the men later?" Nancy asked.

"No, I may be a pirate, but I'm not heartless," Becca said. "I didn't want innocent people suffering from thirst or starvation if they weren't found in time. Lee Po wanted their yachts, I wanted their blood, but we didn't want anyone to die."

"So when you discovered that Cutler had the right blood type," Nancy speculated, "you kidnapped him from the Pecks' house and brought him here."

Becca chuckled. "That was fun. I felt as if we were in a movie and I was the heroine, creeping up in the middle of the night. We planned the operation so well, it came off as smooth as ice cream."

"It may have been fun for *you*," Cutler muttered. "I am not your father, but if you thought I was, why in blazes did you dump me here to sweat for days on this lousy, stinking island?"

"You were treated very well until you made the

mistake of trying to run away," Becca said, growing angry again. "It was your own fault."

"When Mr. Cutler tried to escape, we were up in the mountains," Nancy said. "Was that why Lee Po called you at Casa Maya? Is that why you had to get back to the coast so quickly?"

"Yes," Becca admitted. "I realized I couldn't postpone this . . . this meeting any longer. I was scared—he had almost gotten away. I knew I had to face my father at last."

"Is that why you went on the trip with us?" Nancy asked. "You had to work up the courage to confront him?"

"Maybe." Becca's chin went up, as if she were too proud to admit her weakness. "I also wanted to keep an eye on you, Nancy. As soon as David told me you were a detective—you should have heard him boasting about how many cases you'd solved—I had to make sure you weren't figuring out what was really going on."

Nancy felt the rope around her wrist give a bit. With just a little more slack, her hands would be free. She was covered with perspiration from the heat, and it made her skin slippery—easier to slide out from the cords.

She thought about David, alone in the plane. By now he'd know they were in trouble. The question was, what would he do? She prayed he'd radio for help and wait for the police or the Coast Guard to arrive instead of trying to rescue them himself.

"All right, young lady, you've told your story." Cutler tried to stand up but fell back on the cot, landing awkwardly on his side. "Why not just admit you've made a mistake and let us go?"

"I have not made a mistake!" Becca shouted. "You are my father—and you're going to admit it." She pulled a piece of paper out of her pocket. "I want you to sign this now."

"What is it?" Cutler asked, frowning.

"It states that I am your daughter and you acknowledge me as your heir," Becca said, stamping her foot.

"I'll do no such thing," Cutler roared.

"I've been poor all my life," Becca said, "and you've been throwing money around, buying fancy yachts and wining and dining countless women. Until we started selling the yachts, I never had an extra dime to spend."

"Ah-ha!" Cutler shouted. "Now we get down to the nitty-gritty. You want money! You don't care who your father is. You think you can take me for a sucker, based on this stupid story you've made up. You're nothing but a fortune hunter."

"How dare you!" Becca strode over to him, her hand raised, ready to slap his face.

"Becca, don't!" Nancy cried.

Becca lowered her hand reluctantly. Suddenly she grabbed Cutler by the arm and pulled him up to stand beside her. "Look at us, Nancy. Look at us together. We're a lot alike, aren't we?"

Nancy studied the two. They were both short and fine-boned, with the same stubborn square-cut jaws, and they were both passionately intense people. "I have to admit, I do see a resemblance," Nancy said slowly.

"I look like him." Becca shook Cutler's arm. "And I look like Veronique, too."

"Veronique?" Cutler turned pale. "Is that your mother's name?"

"Yes!" Becca hissed. "Your wife, Veronique. You remember her. She's from the island of Guadeloupe." Becca laughed wildly. "Ramón doesn't know how right he was. He guessed I had a mixture of Northern European, Native American, African, and Spanish blood. He got the first three right, but my mother was part French, not Spanish." She shook Cutler's arm again. "Admit it! You remember Veronique."

"Yes, years ago, but we were only married a short while and *there was no baby.*" Cutler was rigid with tension.

"You forced her to give me away," Becca said.

"I'd never do that," Cutler shouted. "I tell you, there was no baby to give up. Somehow you found her, and you decided to pass yourself off as my daughter. All you want is my money!"

"Why, you despicable toad." Becca pushed Cutler hard against his chest, and he fell back on the cot. She dashed to the door and ran out.

"Are you okay, Mr. Cutler?" Nancy felt the rope around her wrists give way more. Another few seconds and her hands would be free.

"I-I'm fine." He struggled to sit up. "She's—"
Becca came back into the hut. There was a

141

guard behind her carrying a heavy box. "Put it there, Juan," she ordered, pointing to the floor near Nancy.

The guard put the box down and left, closing the door behind him. To Nancy's horror, Becca opened the box and held up a stick of dynamite.

"Now, Daddy dearest," Becca said. "I'll prove to you that I'm not a cheap little fortune hunter. And I am not kidding around." She pulled a pack of matches from her pocket.

"Becca, you can't do that," Nancy shouted. "You'll kill us all!"

"Admit I'm your daughter," she told Cutler.

"You're out of your mind," Cutler said.

Nancy's hands were almost free, but the rope was caught on her knuckles.

Becca pulled off a match and held it to the striking pad. "You have one last chance, Dad."

"You're crazy!" Cutler shouted.

Becca struck the match. A spark flared and died. Becca tore off another match and struck it viciously across the pad. "Admit I'm your daughter!"

"Becca, stop!" Nancy demanded. "Think what you're doing."

The second match refused to spark in the humid air.

Becca tore off another. It burst into flame.

Chapter

Fifteen

B ECCA, DON'T!" NANCY SHOUTED.

Becca dropped the pack of matches and held up the dynamite, bringing the flame close to the wick.

Nancy wrenched her hands free, not caring that the rope scraped her knuckles raw. She threw herself at Becca, knocking the dynamite out of her hand. The stick bounced into the corner.

Becca grunted as Nancy wrapped her arms around the petite girl. They both crashed to the floor, and Becca's match went out. Becca jabbed at Nancy's eyes but missed.

Nancy was thrown off balance trying to avoid the jab, and Becca slid out of her grasp. Becca lunged at the box and grabbed another stick of dynamite.

"You can't stop me!" Becca screamed. She scrabbled around on the floor and found the matchbook she'd dropped. She held the matchbook high, threatening to strike another match.

Nancy reached for her arm. Becca brought the side of her hand down in a vicious karate chop. Nancy felt a flash of pain in her elbow.

Suddenly Becca was sprawled facedown on the floor with Ned on top of her. Though his hands were tied, he'd managed to block her attack with his shoulder. She squirmed furiously, trying to wriggle out from under him.

"Hurry, I can't hold her down," Ned shouted.

Nancy grabbed one of the gags they'd dropped earlier. She caught one of Becca's flailing arms, then the other, and held them behind her back. Quickly she wrapped the cloth around both wrists.

A moment later, Becca lay on the floor defeated, her hands tied behind her, sobbing.

Nancy ignored her while she untied Ned and Robert Cutler. She kept expecting Lee Po or one of the guards to burst in, but no one came.

While Ned and Cutler rubbed their sore wrists and Becca cried into the dirt floor, Nancy cautiously opened the door. Three new boats were in the lagoon, one of them sporting the familiar red stripe of the U.S. Coast Guard. An officer with a bullhorn directed the men in uniform who swarmed over Cutler's captured yacht. The Chinese crew was lined up on the shore under guard. Lee Po stood among them, his head held high.

David and two police officers were searching the huts, one by one.

Nancy closed the door. "We only have a minute, Becca. Stop crying. I want to find out the truth before you're arrested."

"Arrested?" Becca stared up at Nancy.

"Of course," Nancy said briskly. "You're guilty of a crime. You're going to have to pay for it."

"Noooo!" Becca wailed. "I only wanted to find my father."

Nancy went over and helped her sit up. "Now, what is the truth? Is Mr. Cutler really your father, or have you cooked up a little scheme to get his money?"

"He *is* my father. *He is, he is!*" Becca insisted.

Nancy looked at Robert Cutler standing silently beside the cot. "Mr. Cutler?"

"She's exactly like Veronique," he said quietly. "I'd almost forgotten. I loved her so much."

"Then why did you give her up?" Becca asked, some of her spunk returning. "And me?"

"I didn't know about you," Cutler said. "She didn't say a word."

"Mr. Cutler," Nancy said, "do you mean that when you divorced your wife you didn't know she was expecting a baby?"

"I had no idea," he answered. He shook his head, watching his daughter sadly. "Veronique must have made up that story about my forcing her to put you up for adoption."

"Why would she?" Becca demanded.

"Veronique was just like you," Cutler said. "She was very proud, very passionate. Maybe she wanted to keep you away from me. Once you'd found her, she probably wanted you all to herself."

"But she's dead now," Becca said, tears beginning to flow again. "Why did you divorce her?" she finally asked.

"It was an impossible situation. We were just too different. We loved each other, but we simply could not live together. We tried, believe me. We just couldn't make it work." Cutler bowed his head.

"The least you could have done was give her enough money to live a decent life," Becca said with bitterness.

"I couldn't!" Cutler said. "She walked out the door and vanished. I even hired a private detective to look for her, but she'd completely disappeared. I thought she might have returned home to Guadeloupe, but we searched there and found no trace of her."

"Why did she give me up for adoption?" Becca wailed.

"She would have kept you if she could have," Cutler said gently. "When you found her, she accepted you, didn't she?"

Tears poured down Becca's cheeks. "She—she said she loved me—and the adoption was the hardest thing she'd ever done."

They all fell silent. Outside, men shouted orders and boat engines roared. Finally Cutler sighed. "I have plenty of money, and whatever it takes, I'll hire you the best defense lawyer I can find, Becca. I'll do anything to help you now that I know you're mine."

"Thank you, Daddy," Becca said softly.

A week later Nancy, Ned, and Manny were having tea on the screened veranda at Casa Playa, watching the rain pour down in solid sheets.

"It looks like we made that scuba dive at the Blue Hole just in time," Manny said. "The rainy season has arrived."

"It's been a terrific week," Nancy said, nibbling a buttery biscuit. After they had given their testimony to the police and the Coast Guard, their days had been filled with parties, trips to the baboon and jaguar sanctuaries, and visits to different diving spots on the reef. Now they were enjoying a day of relaxation before Nancy and Ned had to return home.

David came out onto the veranda. "Any news about Becca?" Nancy asked him.

David sat down and helped himself to a cookie. "Mr. Cutler told my father he's found a top lawyer for her. He's also offered to help pay for the loss of the first two hijacked yachts if the owners won't press charges."

"That may mean she'll get a lighter sentence," Nancy said, "but she's still going to have to serve time in prison. Piracy is a serious crime."

Ned shook his head in wonder. "Who would

have guessed that sweet little Becca was behind the whole thing?"

"I have to admit, she's a clever actress to have carried off that heiress role," Nancy offered.

"Oh, I almost forgot," David said. "My parents are talking about inviting the boy, Chang, to live here with us. His only relative is his uncle, Lee Po, and he'll be away in prison for quite a while."

"What a great idea," Nancy said. "You can be a big brother to Chang."

"Yeah," David said. "I'll try to keep him away from bad influences, like maverick Mayans." He slapped Manny on the back.

"I want you to know, I've reformed," Manny said with dignity. "The parrot fish are safe from my speargun, at least for a while. I have an appointment to talk to the head of Coastal Zone Management. He was impressed by the letter David helped me write, so I guess I'll try to make changes the legal way. At least I'll give it a go. In the meantime, I've heard there's a gang smuggling jaguarundis over the border."

"What's a jaguarundi?" Ned asked.

"It's a small wildcat," Manny said. "They're very rare, and this gang is too clever for the patrols. I thought I'd see what I could do about it."

"You're hopeless," David said with a grin. "You never give up, do you?"

"Speaking of wildcats," Ned said. "You were wrong about one thing, Nancy. Becca isn't a jaguar *kitten,* she's a full-grown cat—beautiful, but wild at heart. She came so close to blowing us up with that dynamite."

"I'm not sure she meant to light it," Nancy said. "Maybe it was only a threat. Then again, maybe not." She smiled at Ned and placed her hand over his. "But I'm glad that you've learned where dangerous wild animals belong."

Ned pulled her onto his lap and hugged her. "Yes, out in the wilds, not in my arms, like you, Detective Nancy Drew!"

Nancy's next case:

Nancy has come to Westbridge, Massachusetts, nestled in the Berkshire Mountains, to attend a world-famous piano competition. Soon after her arrival she discovers that one of the finalists, Ted Martinelli, has set his sights on something other than first prize. He has his eye on Nancy, and he's playing a very romantic tune. But for Nancy, the urgent question is: will Ted survive the competition? Each of the three finalists has faced a deliberate and mysterious threat, and Nancy knows it's only a matter of time before one of them is hurt . . . or worse. She's uncovered a symphony of sabotage, ambition, and blackmail —and the climax could prove deadly . . . in *Love Notes,* Case #109 in The Nancy Drew Files™.

NANCY DREW® AND THE HARDY BOYS®
TEAM UP FOR MORE MYSTERY... MORE THRILLS...AND MORE EXCITEMENT THAN EVER BEFORE!

A NANCY DREW AND HARDY BOYS SUPERMYSTERY™

- ☐ DOUBLE CROSSING — 74616-2/$3.99
- ☐ A CRIME FOR CHRISTMAS — 74617-0/$3.99
- ☐ SHOCK WAVES — 74393-7/$3.99
- ☐ DANGEROUS GAMES — 74108-X/$3.99
- ☐ THE LAST RESORT — 67461-7/$3.99
- ☐ THE PARIS CONNECTION — 74675-8/$3.99
- ☐ BURIED IN TIME — 67463-3/$3.99
- ☐ MYSTERY TRAIN — 67464-1/$3.99
- ☐ BEST OF ENEMIES — 67465-X/$3.99
- ☐ HIGH SURVIVAL — 67466-8/$3.99
- ☐ NEW YEAR'S EVIL — 67467-6/$3.99
- ☐ TOUR OF DANGER — 67468-4/$3.99
- ☐ SPIES AND LIES — 73125-4/$3.99
- ☐ TROPIC OF FEAR — 73126-2/$3.99
- ☐ COURTING DISASTER — 78168-5/$3.99
- ☐ HITS AND MISSES — 78169-3/$3.99
- ☐ EVIL IN AMSTERDAM — 78173-1/$3.99
- ☐ DESPERATE MEASURES — 78174-X/$3.99
- ☐ PASSPORT TO DANGER — 78177-4/$3.99
- ☐ HOLLYWOOD HORROR — 78181-2/$3.99
- ☐ COPPER CANYON CONSPIRACY — 88514-6/$3.99
- ☐ DANGER DOWN UNDER — 88460-3/$3.99
- ☐ DEAD ON ARRIVAL — 88461-1/$3.99

THE HARDY BOYS CASEFILES